## "What's your objection to me?"

The direct, unexpected question disconcerted Joanna. "I don't have to give you a reason," she said.

Stephen stared at her for a long moment, then gave her a sudden broad smile. "But it would be the polite thing to do, wouldn't it?"

That smile left her breathless. It transformed his hard features, made him seem younger.

"All right," she said at last. "Since you insist, my main objection to you is that you're a policeman. I made up my mind after Ross was killed that I'd never let one into my life again."

He smiled again, more thinly this time. "I'm not asking you to marry me," he said, "only out to dinner."

**ROSEMARY HAMMOND** lives on the West Coast but has traveled extensively with her husband throughout the United States, Mexico and Canada. She loves to write and has been fascinated by the mechanics of fiction ever since her college days. She reads extensively, enjoying everything from Victorian novels to mysteries, spy stories and, of course, romances.

## Books by Rosemary Hammond

# ROSEMARY HAMMOND

## my destiny

*Harlequin Books*

TORONTO • NEW YORK • LONDON
AMSTERDAM • PARIS • SYDNEY • HAMBURG
STOCKHOLM • ATHENS • TOKYO • MILAN

Harlequin Presents first edition September 1990
ISBN 0-373-11296-3

Original hardcover edition published in 1989
by Mills & Boon Limited

# CHAPTER ONE

JOANNA sat at her desk staring down at the letter she had received that morning from the solicitor in Baltimore. After rereading it for the third time, she frowned and glanced at her watch. It was almost ten o'clock. There wouldn't be time to discuss it with Mr Morgan before the meeting, but she'd better call it to his attention as soon as possible. A threatened lawsuit against the hotel was not to be taken lightly.

She got up from the desk, smoothed down the skirt of her blue linen suit, ran a hand over her neatly cut dark hair, then walked across the hall to her employer's office. Inside was a small reception area with a desk set squarely in the middle against the far wall, surrounded by three comfortable-looking chairs, a low table with various magazines spread out neatly on top, and the perennial potted palm, which was virtually a fixture in every Florida interior.

Seated at the desk was Edward Morgan's secretary, a plump woman in her forties with a heavy layer of make-up on her round face and a spectacular head of bright red hair that was twisted and curled into an elaborate coiffure.

'Good morning, Betty. I know it's just about time for the meeting, but something has come up. Is Mr Morgan in?'

The redhead shook her head and made a face. 'He's already left for his golf game. It's Thursday, remember?'

'Right. How could I forget? I take it he doesn't intend even to put in an appearance at the meeting this morning?'

Betty shrugged her plump shoulders and got up from her desk. 'Did you really expect him to? You know how he feels about his sacred golf day.' She smiled. 'Why else do you imagine he made you his assistant?'

'I can't say I blame him. My desk is piled high with work, and I don't particularly relish the thought of sitting through a long speech myself. What is it this time?'

'Oh, the local police are giving us a talk on crime prevention.'

A familiar knot began to tighten in the pit of Joanna's stomach. Now she remembered. It was to be a presentation given jointly by the Pensacola and Panama City Police Departments on ways to avoid the burglaries that had plagued the area for the past few months. The notice had been on the bulletin board for weeks. She must have deliberately pushed it out of her mind.

'That's right,' she said carefully. 'I must have forgotten.'

'Well, there have been all these robberies lately,' Betty said. 'And I suppose it's really our duty at least to listen to what they have to say.'

Joanna started edging towards the door. 'You know, I don't see why both of us have to go, Betty. I really do have tons of work . . .'

Betty rose to her feet and stared at her. 'Edward is counting on you to attend, Joanna,' she said quietly. 'And I think it would be good for you, too. Show yourself you can do it.'

Joanna frowned down at her feet, struggling inwardly. Betty probably had a point. She couldn't keep running away every time the police were even mentioned, especially when it was part of her job.

'All right,' she said at last, forcing out a smile. 'If we have to go, we'd better get started. I'll catch Mr Morgan later.'

They went out into the wide corridor which led to the ballroom down at the far end where the meeting was to be held. Several latecomers were also hurrying towards it, local merchants for the most part, taking time off from their busy schedules to attend.

The large room was already crowded when they got there. It was also quite noisy, with several conversations all going on at once and echoing loudly in the bare, high-ceilinged room. The caretakers had set up folding chairs facing the bandstand that morning, and most of them were taken.

As the two women made their way down the centre aisle, searching for two chairs together, Joanna spotted a stocky, sandy-haired man standing about half-way down and beckoning to them.

'Come on, Betty. It looks as though Martin has saved us a couple of seats.'

By the time they had shuffled awkwardly past the knees of the others in that row and sat down, the first speaker had appeared on the stage. He began to test the microphone for sound, and the room gradually quietened down.

Martin leaned over to speak in Joanna's ear. 'It seems they've dragged old Chief Anderson from Panama City out of retirement for this unrewarding chore.'

Joanna flicked him a quick smile, then turned her eyes forward as the fat, balding policeman in his fifties embarked on a long-winded dissertation on the necessity of installing better alarm systems, putting stronger locks on doors, and several other protective measures that every single person in the audience had probably already implemented years ago.

Joanna had heard it all before, and the man's delivery was so boring, his voice so monotonous, that it wasn't long before her tight muscles unwound and the old anxiety receded. As she relaxed, she began to let her thoughts wander to the various tasks she still had ahead of her that day, ticking them off one by one in her mind as the chief droned on and on.

When he finally wound down there was a light spattering of applause, and the next speaker rose from his seat at the back of the stage and came forward to the microphone.

Betty muttered beside her, 'I suppose this one is going to warn us not to take candy from strangers.'

Joanna suppressed a giggle and glanced towards the stage to see what was going to be inflicted on them next. 'Who is he?' she asked.

'Beats me,' Betty replied. 'I can't tell without my glasses.'

'That's Stephen Ryan,' Martin put in. 'He's a lieutenant in the Pensacola Police Department.'

'Oh, sure,' Betty said. 'I know Stephen. He's a local boy.'

Martin laughed. 'Hardly a boy. He was three years ahead of me in school, and that puts him in his late thirties. He's now the Pensacola Police Department's blue-eyed boy, from what I hear, one of those dedicated men who don't know the meaning of fear.'

Joanna sobered instantly at the reminder, and the sickening ache tightened in her chest once again. Ross had been just such a policeman, with just that kind

f dedication and courage, and eventually it had cost
im his life. She clasped her hands together in her lap
nd stiffened in her chair, staring straight ahead at
he man on the stage.

He was standing there quietly, waiting for the buzz
f conversation to stop. He seemed perfectly relaxed,
tall man with black hair, dressed in a well-fitting
ark suit, white shirt and striped tie. As Joanna gazed
ixedly at him, he seemed vaguely familiar to her,
lthough she couldn't place him. Possibly he'd been
friend of Ross's. But she didn't want to think about
hat.

His hands hung loosely at his sides as he gazed out
t the audience, a slightly sardonic expression on his
ean, tanned face, as though he was about to address
classroom of unruly children.

Then, abruptly, he began to speak, his low, clear
oice rising above the background hum, which in-
tantly subsided at the first words he uttered.

'I've come here today,' he stated in a cold, clipped
oice, 'to tell you that the major cause of crime in
his area is you, the merchants, business men and
vomen, professionals.'

The whole audience seemed to gasp in unison, and
here was a sudden hush in the room. The man paused
or a second or two to let his words sink in, then went
n.

'Chief Anderson has just told you what you could
o to keep out the thieves who might break in, and
know most of you have already taken those pre-
autions. What I'm going to tell you about is some-
hing quite different—the thieves under your own
oof.'

There were still murmurings from the audience, and
e raised his voice. 'Each one of you manages a

business or provides a service. That usually means you need to hire some kind of help.'

He glanced around the silent room, as though searching for disguised criminals, then, to her horror, his narrowed gaze fixed firmly on Joanna.

'You, for example,' his voice rang out. 'Do you know the backgrounds of all the people working for you?'

As his stony gaze bored into her, a warm tide of embarrassment flowed over her, and she had to make an effort not to fidget in her chair. Was that a rhetorical question, or did he expect an answer?

Then her discomfort began to give way to anger. What right did he have to put her on the spot like that? She lifted her chin, ready to do battle with the man right there in front of everybody, but before she could get a word out he had shifted his gaze to another unhappy victim.

'Or you?' he said, pointing at the local undertaker.

Joanna closed her eyes and slumped back in her chair, weak with relief and hardly listening to him as he went on in that vein for ten more minutes, warning them that they all needed to exercise constant vigilance over their own people, especially the transients, the floaters who showed up out of nowhere.

'Get references,' he commanded sternly. 'Then check them.'

When he was through, he nodded briefly at the audience, then, without waiting for any reaction, questions or applause, he strode off the stage and stepped lightly down the three stairs that led to the main floor.

There was dead silence in the large room. Then pandemonium broke out, and he disappeared into the crowd that now rose from their seats in a body and

clustered around him. Joanna could hear snatches of
conversation, voices raised in indignation. 'If you
think I'm going to suspect my own people of robbing
me...' was the general tenor.

Joanna looked at Betty, who raised her heavily
pencilled eyebrows heavenwards. 'Edward's not going
to like that!' she said.

'It doesn't sound to me as though anyone else did,
either,' Joanna commented drily. 'Just listen to them.
No wonder he quit so abruptly.'

'He's right, though, you know,' Martin put in.
'Take it from me. As a lawyer, I can assure you that
most crimes, at least around here, and probably in
most predominantly tourist areas, are inside jobs. As
he said, beware of transients.'

They got up from their seats and made their way
towards the aisle, crowded now, as everyone apparently decided to leave at once.

'Edward still isn't going to like it,' Betty repeated.
'He's got a fetish about trusting the people who work
for him.'

'Well, he's been warned,' Martin said.

'He's also very careful about the people he hires,'
Joanna said. 'I should know. He does require references, and believe me, I check out every one of them.'

They were out in the wide main corridor now.
Martin stopped and turned to her. 'Well, he'll
probably be all right, then.' He glanced at his watch.
'I've got to be on my way. I have a court appearance
at one-thirty.'

'Do you have just a few minutes?' Joanna asked.
'There's something I'd like to discuss with you, a letter
I received this morning from a former guest threat-
ening a lawsuit.'

He smiled at her, his gaze softening. 'I'd do just about anything for you, Joanna, you know that. But I really do have to run. Can it wait until tomorrow?'

'Sure. I'm sure there's no emergency. I want to get Mr Morgan's opinion anyway.' She laughed. 'Although I know he'll just tell me to turn it over to you, as the hotel's solicitor. I thought I might surprise him and do that before I got the order.'

'I'll call you tomorrow, then.'

'Fine.'

With a little wave he turned to go, but in the next instant he stopped short, staring straight ahead of him over Joanna's shoulder. Then he suddenly broke into a wide grin.

'Here comes the star turn now,' he said. 'Our valiant hero in the flesh.'

Without thinking, Joanna turned around to see the tall policeman heading directly towards them, striding leisurely ahead of the dispersing crowd, his hands in his trouser-pockets. Their eyes met and held briefly. Caught for an instant in that steady blue stare, Joanna couldn't move. Then the colour flooded into her face and she quickly turned back, hoping to make her escape before he could reach them.

But it was too late. By then Martin had already raised his hand in a salute, and before she could make her move she was being introduced to him.

'Joanna, this is Stephen Ryan. *Lieutenant* Stephen Ryan now, I believe,' he added with a smile. 'One of Pensacola's finest, defender of truth, right and justice.'

Joanna looked up at the man and gave him a cool nod. 'I'm impressed,' she said drily. 'I'm also surprised you got out of there without being lynched.'

He flashed her a thin, sardonic half-smile. 'You sound as though you'd like to be first in line. Perhaps hold the rope.'

She flared at that. 'I just don't appreciate being singled out like that,' she snapped. 'Is that considered effective police technique? Badgering innocent people?'

He raised one heavy dark eyebrow. 'Didn't you even listen to what I had to say?' He shook his head. 'My whole point was that it's often the innocent people who invite crime.'

'There's still no need to be offensive about it,' she said huffily.

'I'm sorry you found it offensive,' he said stiffly. 'It's not personal, you know. I just pick a few faces at random and pin them down.' The smile widened. 'But I do find it gets people's attention.'

Joanna turned to Martin and Betty. 'I've got tons of work to do,' she said, still nettled. 'Think I'll go on ahead now.'

'I'll come with you,' Betty said. She nodded at Lieutenant Ryan. 'Nice to see you again, Stephen.'

As the two women walked on down the hall together away from the men, Joanna had the uneasy sensation that Lieutenant Ryan's bright blue eyes were following her every step of the way, and when they reached Betty's office she quickly followed her inside.

'What was that all about?' asked Betty in a bewildered tone.

Joanna turned to face her. 'Oh, I don't know,' she replied irritably. 'It just annoyed me to have him put me on the spot back there when he was giving his stupid speech.'

'I didn't think it was so stupid,' Betty protested. 'You're not being fair. He's only doing his job, after all.' She fixed Joanna with an appraising eye. 'Listen, there's more to it than that, isn't there?'

Joanna stared at her for a moment, then sighed heavily. 'You might be right. Maybe I was being unfair. I guess I still react badly to policemen.' She smiled. 'Let's just forget it. Will you be sure to tell Mr Morgan about that letter when he gets back?'

'Sure, but I don't see why you need his advice,' the redhead said. Then she added gruffly, 'Seems to me you're doing pretty well on your own. At least as far as your job is concerned.' She put a hand on Joanna's arm and gave her a knowing smile. 'But how's your love-life?'

Joanna laughed. 'My love-life? What kind of question is that? As you're well aware, I don't have any love-life.'

'You know, you really ought to think about getting married again,' Betty said in a serious tone. 'You're still young, still attractive. You have your whole life ahead of you. I can't see you spending it managing other people's hotels.'

'Well, you're one to talk! I don't see you rushing to the altar.'

Betty waved a well-manicured hand in the air. 'Oh, me. I'm over the hill, not as young as I used to be. I'm also already a two-time loser. But you really should consider it. I'm serious.'

'Thanks, Betty, but I'm honestly not in the market. I don't know. After Ross was killed I just lost interest in matrimony.'

'You're not still in mourning, are you?' Betty asked. 'Surely not after three years?'

'Oh, no. Nothing like that.'

She was becoming uncomfortable with the conversation and was relieved when the telephone on the desk suddenly started buzzing and Betty reached out to answer it.

'Mr Morgan's office.' She listened for a moment, then said, 'She's right here,' and handed the receiver to Joanna.

'Joanna Barnes,' she said into the telephone.

'Can you come to the front desk right away?' came the tight voice of Andy Thompson, the daytime receptionist. 'We have a little problem.'

'I'll be right there,' she said quickly, and hung up.

Betty raised an enquiring eyebrow. 'Trouble?'

Joanna shrugged. 'Constantly. It's the name of the game in hotel management.'

'Andy sounded upset.'

'Andy's a good receptionist, but he's inclined to fall apart when things don't run perfectly smoothly.'

With a little wave she went out into the wide corridor that led to the hotel lobby. What was called for was her calmest, most professional manner.

The problem turned out to be an irate elderly couple from Cleveland who had spent two weeks at the Miramar Hotel every May for the three years Joanna had worked there; it hinged on a mix-up in their reservations.

'We *always* have that corner room facing the Gulf,' the indignant wife declared loudly, and Joanna knew that only a drastic measure would placate her.

She turned to Andy, who stood behind the desk virtually quivering with nervous anxiety. 'Give Mr and Mrs Goldman Room 3C for tonight, Andy, and there will be no charge. Tomorrow we'll move them into their regular room.'

Andy widened his eyes at her and opened his mouth to protest, but Joanna silenced him with a look and turned back to the Goldmans with a smile.

'I hope that will be satisfactory,' she said pleasantly.

It was obvious from the pleased look on their faces that it was, indeed, more than satisfactory, and Joanna watched them leave with a sigh of relief. Then she turned to face a red-faced Andy.

'Listen, Andy,' she said gently, 'Mr Morgan pounded it into me from the day I started working for him that the only rigid rule he had was that the comfort and convenience of the guests always comes first. Now, what we'll do is move the occupants of the Goldmans' room into a top-floor suite at no extra cost.'

The young man goggled at her. 'But—but...' he spluttered helplessly. 'A suite will cost twice what they're paying now.'

'You have to look at the long-term view,' she explained patiently. 'The suite is empty anyway. It won't cost us anything to give it to them and the Goldmans will get the room they want. Everyone will be happy, and that means future business for the hotel.'

Andy shook his head and gave her a grudging smile. 'I never would have thought of that, Joanna. Guess that's why I'm the receptionist and you're the manager.'

'You'll learn,' she said firmly. 'I wasn't born knowing how to deal with these little crises, you know. Edward Morgan has been a wonderful teacher.'

At least *that* problem was solved. Until the next one came along. Several did, of course, and it wasn't until eight o'clock that night, after a late supper in the dining-room, that she was finally ready to call it a day.

Leaving the main building, she went out through the back entrance of the hotel and up the path to her own small cottage on the grounds. It was dusk by now and raining gently, a light spring shower that was reflected in a shimmering curtain by the bright lights shining out from the hotel, and, even running the last few yards, she was still dripping when she reached her front door.

The cottage was quite small—only a living-room, bedroom, bathroom and tiny kitchenette—but pleasant and compact, and since Joanna spent most of her time at the hotel, and took all of her meals there, it was more than adequate for her needs.

Once inside, she stripped off her wet clothes, got into a warm bath, and firmly tuned the day's problems out of her mind. As she soaked, she thought over her conversation with Betty that afternoon, wondering what had prompted it.

Suddenly a wave of self-doubt swept over her. Did she really appear to other people as a still-grieving widow? Was she wrong to concentrate all her energies on her job? Could she help it if she wasn't interested in romance?

After she'd dried off and put on her nightclothes, a sudden urge struck Joanna to call her parents. Not for advice, she told herself, but just to hear the sound of their voices. She wrote to them faithfully once a week and tried to get to Boston for a visit at least once a year, but she hadn't spoken to them for weeks.

She glanced at her watch. It was only nine o'clock, still early. As she made for the telephone in her bedroom, she could picture them in her mind, her father settled behind the evening paper or watching a ball game on television, her mother sitting nearby working on the stuffed animals that had become so popular and sold so well in the local department stores.

Her mother answered the telephone, and when she heard the familiar voice Joanna was surprised to feel tears sting her eyes.

'Mother,' she said. 'It's Joanna.'

'Darling, how lovely to hear from you.' Joanna heard her call out to her father that his daughter was on the telephone. 'Is anything wrong?' she said when she got back to her.

'No. Not a thing. I haven't talked to you for quite a while, and just thought I'd check in with you.'

'How's the job going?'

'Quite well. Mr Morgan gives me more responsibility all the time, and I really like what I'm doing. How are things in Boston?'

Her mother launched into a long recitation about the unseasonably cold spring they'd had, and her father's law practice, which seemed to be thriving and far more than he could handle alone, until finally she ran out of breath.

'Other than that,' she wound up, 'things are pretty much the same.' She paused for a moment, then said cautiously, 'How are you and Martin Kingsley getting along?'

Joanna almost laughed out loud. She knew quite well that her mother had been nursing the secret hope that somehow Joanna and Martin would fall in love and marry, almost from the moment she heard the news of Ross's death. An incurable romantic, and happily married for almost thirty years, she couldn't comprehend how any woman would not prefer wedded bliss to a career.

'Oh, Martin's fine. Same old Martin, as a matter of fact.'

'No—um—*developments* in that direction?' her mother asked cautiously.

'No, Mother, I told you a long time ago that even if I were interested in romance—which I'm not—Martin Kingsley is probably the last person on earth I'd get involved with.'

'He seems like such a nice young man,' her mother murmured. 'I don't mean to interfere in your life, darling, but both your father and I would feel much better about you if you were to marry again. After all, a career isn't everything.'

'Well, it is to me—at least until I get swept off my feet, and I don't see any immediate chance of that happening.'

They chatted for a while longer, and she spoke briefly to her father, who hated talking on the telephone, then they said goodbye, with promises to call again soon.

After hanging up, Joanna felt a little better about herself and a little less confused. Even though her mother was still set on marrying her off again, just talking with her parents, reminding herself of their very existence, provided a ballast that gave her a more secure sense of her own identity.

She had meant what she'd said to her mother about her career coming first right now. And as for the likelihood that any man would sweep her off her feet, it was really laughable.

She reached into her desk and took out a worn photograph album from the bottom drawer. Her wedding pictures were in there, and she turned the pages slowly until she came to her favourite, the one where she in her white bridal gown and Ross, resplendent in his dress uniform, were cutting the cake.

We were so young, she thought, and so happy. Now it all seemed like a dream. Looking at Ross's open, boyish face now, three years after his death, he seemed almost like a stranger to her, yet the sight of him brought back so many painful memories of the way he was killed, knifed by a panicky drug addict, that she could hardly bear it.

She forced her eyes back to the photograph, and immediately the image of the handsome young police officer gradually altered in her mind until once again he became that white, still figure lying helpless in the hospital bed just before he died, his young, healthy body swathed in bandages, the hopeless look on the doctor's face as he told her there wasn't a chance he would survive the wound in his chest.

She closed her eyes and leaned her head back on the chair as the waves of anxiety rolled over her once again. It had been terrible to lose her young husband, but even worse was the aftermath, the near total collapse she'd suffered when it had really sunk in that she was all alone, that she would no longer have his strength to rely on. Her first instinct had been to run home to her parents, to bury herself under their sheltering roof again.

But her mother, wisely, would have none of that. 'You're twenty-two years old, Joanna, a grown woman,' she'd said sternly. 'And you've got to get control of yourself, make a new life for yourself.'

She remembered, too, the bitterness she'd felt at the time. It was her parents, after all, who had raised their only child in such a sheltered environment that she hadn't felt able to stand on her own two feet after Ross was killed. Then they didn't even want her to come home. She'd felt so betrayed by them.

Now, of course, after three years of proving she could manage quite well on her own, she could see the wisdom of the stand they'd taken. She just wished they'd done it earlier and taught her to be more independent before she was forced into it by her early widowhood. But that was all water under the bridge now. She *had* done it, after all, and mainly thanks to her job. That had saved her sanity, if not her very life.

She'd been near suicidal for weeks after the funeral. Severe emotional trauma, the doctor had called it when she'd collapsed in the street the first time she'd gone out to a job interview. Only time would heal it, he'd said, and the more she learned to rely on herself, without the crutch of her parents' protection, the sooner she would get her confidence back.

Now, today's encounter with that arrogant, self-righteous policeman had brought it all back, and she simply wouldn't have it. She would never allow herself to be put in that position again. Even though she'd succeeded in making a secure life for herself, without her parents, without her husband, she was still afraid that it could all be swept away in a moment, and she'd be back in that dark tunnel of despair again. It would be so easy.

She slammed the album shut and replaced it hurriedly in the drawer. She couldn't let that happen.

# CHAPTER TWO

SOME time later that very night, Joanna was awakened out of a deep sleep by the piercing sound of a siren wailing into the stillness. She opened her eyes groggily, listening, as the siren grew louder, coming closer now.

She raised up in bed and pulled aside the curtain at the window over her bed to see a blinking blue light moving down the main drive towards the hotel. Finally it stopped directly in front. At the same time, the telephone by the side of her bed started to shrill loudly, and she reached out to snatch it up.

'Joanna, it's Betty,' came the breathless voice. 'There's been an accident, a robbery. Edward has been badly beaten. You'd better get over here right away.'

Fully awake by now, Joanna drew in her breath sharply. For a moment she couldn't speak at all. Her head started to spin, and her heart was pounding wildly.

'Joanna!' came Betty's voice. 'Are you there?'

'Yes,' she said weakly at last. 'I don't understand. What happened?'

'I don't have time to explain it now. The ambulance just got here, and we're waiting for the police. It's a madhouse. All the guests are wandering around in a near-panic, and I need you here, Joanna. Now!'

Betty sounded very near the ragged edge of hysteria, and Joanna forced herself to concentrate on staying calm. Taking a deep breath, she swung her legs over the side of the bed. 'I'll be right there,' she said, and hung up.

Jumping quickly out of bed, she threw on some clothes, then went outside and ran through the light drizzle up the path that led from her cottage to the hotel. All the main-floor lights were blazing. At the front entrance were an ambulance and two police cars, blue lights flicking on and off. People in their night-clothes were milling around under the covered portico, huddled in groups and speaking in hushed tones.

Joanna pushed past them. 'Please,' she said as she went, 'let me through. Won't you all please go back to your rooms? There's nothing you can do here.'

Inside there was more pandemonium, with yet another crowd of gawping guests and several uniformed policemen, who were trying to herd them out of the lobby. As Joanna made her way towards the front desk, a dishevelled Betty came forward to greet her, hands outstretched, her face grey under the layer of make-up.

'How is he?' Joanna asked, taking Betty's hands in hers.

'They say he'll be all right, but he took an awful beating, and the paramedics are getting him ready to take to the hospital.' Her eyes were huge. 'They have to check him for internal injuries and possible skull fracture.'

'What happened?'

'Apparently the night clerk was sick, and Edward took over for him. Didn't want to disturb you. I was in bed asleep up in my room on the second floor, and the noise of the struggle woke me up. When I got down here, Edward was lying on the floor, bleeding. He was barely conscious by then, but just managed to tell me that two masked men had come in with guns and demanded money. Edward put up a fight, the old fool, wouldn't give it to them, so they simply knocked him unconscious and took the money and ran.'

Joanna glanced behind the desk where two white-coated men were kneeling on the floor beside her unconscious employer. She took one look at the silent form lying so still and white on the stretcher and felt her knees grow weak. There was no sign of blood, but he was already heavily bandaged.

At the sight, her head started spinning around and her knees grew weak. It seemed like Ross all over again. Reaching out a hand to support herself on the counter, she took several deep breaths. She had to pull herself together. Too many things depended on her.

She turned to one of the medics. 'How badly is he hurt?' she asked, and was amazed to hear how steady her voice sounded.

The man looked up and gave her a reassuring smile. 'I don't think it's critical,' he said. 'The worst of it is the head wound, and we've got to get him to the hospital right away to check for possible fracture or concussion. He's also lost a lot of blood.'

'I'm going with you,' Betty pronounced flatly. She turned to Joanna. 'OK?'

'Well, it's all right with me, but shouldn't you stay here and talk to the police?'

'I've already told them everything I know. If they need me, they'll know where to find me. I'm not leaving his side.'

Once the ambulance was gone and all the excitement over, the police were finally able to clear the lobby of spectators. One of them questioned Joanna briefly, and after he'd taken her statement, which amounted to nothing at all since she'd been sound asleep throughout the whole thing, she called Andy

Thompson to ask him to take over the rest of the night shift. It was past midnight by now, and she was exhausted.

Andy arrived just as the last policeman went out of the door, and after Joanna had explained to him what had happened she trudged wearily back down the wet path to her cottage. Once inside, she locked and bolted the door behind her, then went into her bedroom and got into her nightclothes again, hoping to get a few hours' sleep before morning, when she'd have to face the day all by herself. With Edward Morgan in the hospital, the whole burden of running the hotel would fall on her shoulders.

Just as she was about to turn out the lights and fall into bed, she heard a car pull up out in front, a door slam, footsteps coming up the path. What now? she wondered. She went back to the living-room window and pulled the curtain aside. Through the misty rain she could just make out the shape of a man walking up the path towards the cottage. After a moment the doorbell rang, and she went into the hall to answer it.

She paused at the door. 'Yes,' she called. 'Who is it?'

'Police,' came a masculine voice.

She unlocked the door, but kept on the chain bolt. How did she know it was really the police? Perhaps the robbers had come back. 'May I see your identification, please?' she said to the fresh-faced young man standing on the other side.

Then, when she took a second look, she felt a little silly. He was obviously a policeman, clearly visible now under the porch light and wearing a crisp starched uniform with a gun belt and a very official-looking badge on his light blue shirt. Not only that, but he had such an open, guileless expression on his boyish face that he couldn't possibly be a criminal.

He held up a plastic identification card with his photograph on it. Patrolman John O'Connor, it said, twenty-three years old, according to his birth date. Satisfied, she shut the door to slide the chain bolt free.

'Come in, Officer,' she said.

It wasn't until she'd opened the door wide to let him in that she saw the other man. He had obviously come up behind the patrolman and had been standing just out of her line of vision, so that she hadn't noticed him in the shadows. Now, as he stepped into the light, she recognised Stephen Ryan.

Her whole body stiffened, and she stared up at him, every muscle tense, gripped by a sudden sensation of anxiety that verged on the edge of fear. He was quite a bit taller than the other man, and dressed in the same dark suit he'd had on that morning. He stood there calmly looking down at her, hatless, the raindrops glistening in his black hair.

Then she heard Patrolman O'Connor's voice, and the spell was broken. 'This is Lieutenant Ryan, ma'am,' he said. 'He's in charge of the case.'

The tall man inclined his head briefly and said, 'Mrs Barnes and I have already met.'

Joanna led them into the living-room. Lieutenant Ryan stood in the middle of the room, his arms folded across his chest, and gave it a cursory glance, gazing through half-closed eyes at the familiar possessions with a critical, appraising eye while the younger policeman took out a notebook and pencil and stood, as though at attention, waiting for orders.

Joanna watched them both covertly. Her earlier impression that there was something familiar about him was even stronger now. As she examined him more closely, feature by feature, he seemed far more attractive than he had that morning when she'd been so irritated at the way he'd embarrassed her during his talk, but also somehow more threatening.

He was taller than she'd realised, for one thing, his hair darker, and he had a more athletic build. Lieutenant Ryan moved with the stealthy ease and grace of a jungle cat rather than a muscle-man.

He had finished his brief inspection by now, and as he turned to face her the thought flashed through her mind that, in spite of her instinctive antipathy, he certainly was an impressive-looking man. And, she added, noting the hard blue eyes and the firm set of the bony jaw, one of the coldest. In any case, he was a policeman, and that put him absolutely off limits for her.

Then it suddenly dawned on her that she was standing in her living-room in the middle of the night in her bathrobe and slippers, her dark hair untidy and streaming down to her shoulders. She clutched her robe together tightly and gave the man a cool, challenging look.

'Why are you here?' she asked.

'I'd like to ask you a few questions about the robbery and shooting, if you feel up to it.'

Although the masked expression on the lean dark face revealed nothing but an official, impersonal curiosity, Joanna was dimly aware of something more than that in the man's steady gaze, a hint of mockery on the thin, unsmiling mouth. Was he laughing at her discomfiture, amused to have caught her looking as though she'd just jumped out of bed?

'I see,' she said in a tight voice. 'I don't know what I can tell you, however, since I was asleep through the whole thing. Can't it wait until tomorrow?'

'Look, Mrs Barnes,' the tall man said sternly, 'I don't have a lot of time. My job is to investigate these incidents, to find out what happened and, hopefully, to put the bad guys behind bars and out of circulation. You should know that without my having to tell you. If you won't talk to me, I can't do that, now, can I?'

Their eyes met then, and Joanna found herself held in their cold blue light. 'I'm sorry,' she murmured. 'I'll do what I can to help you, but I really can't tell you a thing. All I know is what I was told by the others. By the time I got there, the men who'd beaten him were long gone and the police had already arrived.'

'And you have no idea who might have done it?'

She stared at him. 'Of course not. How could I?'

He shrugged. 'As I tried to convince you people earlier today, robberies of this sort are often inside jobs.'

'Are you accusing me of something?'

'No, I'm not. But I thought you might have some ideas for me—a disgruntled employee or relative, a suspicious character hanging around, anything at all that might help us. Sometimes the most insignificant detail will set us on the right track.'

'No,' she said coldly, 'I don't. Mr Morgan is a wonderful man, an ideal employer, and all the staff, without exception, are fanatically loyal to him. It couldn't possibly be anyone who works here. I'd swear to that.'

He stared at her for some moments, then nodded. 'All right. If that's all you can tell me, I guess it will have to do. Although,' he added, 'I'll have to question you again later.'

He beckoned to Patrolman O'Connor then, and Joanna followed them out of the room. When they reached the door, the younger policeman went ahead down the path to the waiting police car, while Lieutenant Ryan lingered behind for a moment.

He reached into the breast pocket of his dark suit jacket, then turned to her and handed her a card. 'This has my office number on it. If you recall anything at all that might be helpful, perhaps you'd let me know.'

With a nod, she took the card from him and started to close the door, but as she gave him one last look something in his expression held her. The corners of his thin mouth were lifted slightly in a brief, quizzical smile.

'It's been a long time, Joanna,' he said quietly. 'How have you been?'

She stared at him. What was he talking about? She'd been introduced to him only that afternoon. Who was he? Where had she seen him before? Then, as she examined him more closely, it dawned on her.

'Stephen Ryan,' she said in a halting voice, as she searched her mind. 'Yes, I do remember now. We have met before. I didn't recognise you this morning. It *has* been a long time.'

'Only three years,' he said, lifting a heavy dark eyebrow. 'Not very flattering to be forgotten so soon.'

She flushed at that and looked away. 'I'm sorry,' she said almost inaudibly. Then she lifted her chin. 'I know that you and my husband were friends. It's nothing personal. It's just that for three years now I've gone to great lengths to put everything about Ross's death out of my mind.'

He nodded. 'Of course. I understand. Sorry to bring back unpleasant memories. He was a good friend, a fine policeman. I was sorry to lose him, too. I never did get a chance to tell you that after the funeral.'

She couldn't think of one thing to say, and after waiting for a moment he said a brief, polite goodnight, then turned to go down the path to the waiting car.

After she had shut the door behind him, she listened to his footsteps going down the path, then the slam of the car door as he got inside and the roar of the motor as they drove away. The house was silent again.

Joanna turned off the lights and once again dragged herself wearily down the hall to her bedroom. She crawled into bed and lay there in the darkness, thinking about Stephen Ryan. A strange man. A compelling man, in his way. She hadn't known him well when Ross was alive, but she did recall that even then he had the reputation of a loner, aloof, set apart.

Was he married? She hadn't noticed a ring. What kind of man was he? Serious, she decided, committed to his job. Ruthless, determined. Was there no softness in him at all? She couldn't picture him as a devoted husband, a doting father. But as a lover?

She laughed aloud in the dark. Who would ever have dreamed she'd ever be attracted to another policeman? She'd come a long way, though. Tonight she'd overcome her fears and managed to function quite capably. Was she completely healed at last?

Possibly, she thought, as she drifted off to sleep. But, as interesting as she found the tall, remote Stephen Ryan, he wasn't worth risking her hard-won independence. No man was.

\*     \*     \*

The next day everything miraculously managed to return to order. As Joanna walked from her cottage to the hotel in the early-morning sunshine, the salty tang of the Gulf of Mexico filling the air, it almost seemed to her as though the dreadful events of the night before had never happened.

After thanking a bleary-eyed and exhausted Andy for holding the fort for her all night, she called the hospital as soon as she got to her office to see how Edward Morgan was. Her call was transferred around several times, but she was finally reassured that he was resting comfortably and out of danger. She hung up and was just about to turn to her morning list of appointments when the telephone rang.

She reached out and picked it up. 'This is Mrs Barnes. May I help you?'

'Joanna?' came a familiar masculine voice.

'Yes.'

'This is Stephen Ryan.'

A vivid image of the tall, stern policeman instantly appeared unbidden in her mind, and a disturbing warmth began to creep over her. With a brief flash of irritation, she dismissed it and sat up a little straighter in her chair.

'Yes, Lieutenant Ryan,' she said coolly. 'What can I do for you?'

'I just called to tell you that I stopped by at the hospital in Pensacola this morning on my way to work to see Edward Morgan, and that he seems to be doing fine.'

'I see,' she said grudgingly. 'Well, thank you for calling and telling me.' Then, unbending a little, she asked lightly, 'Don't you ever sleep?'

There was a dead silence on the line. Then, 'Occasionally,' he said briefly. 'I also wanted you to know that I tried to get him to talk about what happened last night, and made absolutely no headway at all. He won't even discuss the possibility that one of his employees could be involved in the robbery. Now,' he went on briskly, 'you'll have to admit that you were somewhat less than forthcoming yourself last night, and I have a few more questions I'd like to ask you.'

Joanna stiffened. 'I don't understand,' she said. 'Are you telling me that I'm a suspect?'

'I'm a policeman, Mrs Barnes,' came the frosty reply. 'It's my job to suspect everybody.' He paused for a moment. 'But no, you're not a suspect. Your record is impeccable. I couldn't even find a parking ticket.'

He *had* been checking on her, then. 'I see,' she said in an even tone. 'It sounds as though you've done a thorough job. What else did you find out while you were investigating me?'

'That you're twenty-five years old, unmarried, have worked at the Miramar Hotel for three years and are a sound credit risk,' he replied promptly. There was the barest hint of amusement in his voice.

Joanna was speechless. On the one hand she felt as though her privacy had been shamelessly invaded; on the other, she knew he was probably just doing his job. In either case, she couldn't think of one sensible thing to say.

Then he spoke again. 'It's only routine,' he said blandly. 'Nothing personal. I'm still pursuing the line that it was an inside job and, since you seem to be closest to the picture, I thought I'd give it one more try. I'd like to stop by the hotel to interview you again some time later today, if it's convenient.'

'I don't see what good that would do,' she said. 'There's really nothing more I can tell you.' If Edward didn't want to pursue that line, it certainly wasn't up to her to interfere.

'I realise you don't want to involve any of the hotel personnel,' he went on. 'And I appreciate that. But I don't have such scruples. Whoever did this thing has got to be stopped. It may be unpleasant, but that's my job.'

Joanna knew he was right. 'All right,' she said reluctantly. 'But I still don't believe I'll be able to help you.' She glanced down at her afternoon schedule. 'How's three o'clock? I have some free time then.'

'That will be fine.'

After they'd hung up, Joanna sat with her hand on the receiver for a long time, staring into space as she pictured once again in her mind the tall, well-built figure, the cold blue eyes, the stern, remote expression. Then the image of her dead husband as he lay bleeding and wounded in that dark alley flashed into her mind, and somehow the two became commingled.

She gave herself an impatient little shake and picked up her list. It was time to get to work on her busy morning schedule.

Mrs Murphy, the head housekeeper, was first, reporting a normal linen count for the season with the usual number of missing towels, ashtrays and bedding, and Joanna crossed off her name.

Her next appointment was a rather stormy session with Mario, the Italian chef, concerning his running battle with the *maître d'hôtel*, an equally volatile Russian. That one still had yet to be resolved, and after he'd left she pencilled in a question mark after his name.

Her regular weekly meeting with the hotel's accountant was her last appointment of the morning, barring emergencies, and by the time he was gone

Joanna's growling stomach told her she was ready for some fortification before tackling her full afternoon agenda.

After a brief check of the first quarter's figures that he had left with her, she set the balance sheet down on top of the neat pile of folders in the centre of her desk and left for lunch.

The coffee-shop faced towards the beach, and Joanna took her usual table by the window where she could look out upon the wide stretch of sparkling white sand and the bright blue-green of the Gulf of Mexico.

It was early May, not yet the height of the season for the northern Gulf Coast. Its year-round temperatures were much cooler than the cities on the southern tip of Florida, and so it had more attractions for tourists in the summer than the winter. Except for the occasional hurricane, when the winds came screaming across the water, flattening the tall palm trees along the shore and cluttering the immaculate beach with debris picked up on its journey, to Joanna the weather was near-perfect.

'Mind if I join you?' came a familiar voice.

She looked up to see Betty standing beside her table. 'Please do,' she said with a smile.

Betty pulled out a chair and settled herself at the table across from Joanna. 'You seemed so intent on admiring the view when I came in, I almost hated to interrupt you.'

'I never get tired of it,' Joanna admitted. 'It's got to be the most beautiful beach in the world. That sand is so fine it squeaks when you walk on it, and the water so clear you can see the bottom right up to the shore.'

Betty raised an eyebrow and reached for a menu. 'How much does the Florida Chamber of Commerce pay you for your enthusiastic advertising endorsements?'

Joanna laughed. 'My enthusiasm comes from a childhood spent in the north. You can't really appreciate water actually warm enough to swim in comfortably unless you come from a place like Boston.'

'As a Florida native, I bow to your superior knowledge.'

'Is there any fresh news about Mr Morgan? I called the hospital this morning and they told me he was out of danger.'

Betty grinned at her. 'I just came from there, and you can save your sympathy for his doctor and nurses. He's already roaring around like a caged lion.'

'I'd like to run into Pensacola this afternoon to see him. Is there anything he needs?'

'Better not. His main concern is the hotel, and he gave me express orders to forbid you to leave your post for one second while he's away.'

Joanna laughed. 'All right. I'll go tonight, then.'

The waitress came to their table just then and they both ordered. When she'd gone, Joanna looked over at the older woman with a worried frown.

'Lieutenant Ryan called me this morning,' she said slowly. 'He wants to interview me this afternoon. I know he's got this bee in his bonnet about it being an inside job, and I don't know what to say to him.'

'That's easy. Tell him the truth.'

'Well, I know, but there are various ways of telling the truth. I don't want to say anything that might incriminate any of the employees here. I just know none of them could have had any part of it.'

'I don't know that I'd go that far,' Betty said archly. 'Maybe not the beating part. I'll never believe that. But do you really think that Mario or Ivan are incapable of dipping their fingers into the till?'

Joanna stared at her, horrified. 'Betty! I can hardly believe you even think that. What would Mr Morgan say? You know how dead set he is against suspecting the people who work for him.'

Betty gave a sarcastic bark of a laugh. 'Oh, Edward,' she said dismissively. 'He's a babe in the woods as far as his precious employees are concerned. You take my advice and just tell the truth. You don't have to cast suspicion on any one person, but if you know of any hanky-panky that's going on, however minor, you'd better tell the police about it.'

'But I don't know of anything like that.'

'Then there's no problem, is there?'

At three o'clock on the dot there was a sharp knock on Joanna's office door. She got up from her desk and crossed over to open it to Stephen Ryan. Standing beside him was a tall blonde woman in a neat tailored uniform.

'Come in,' Joanna said.

'This is Sergeant Laura Blake,' he said briefly as they went inside. 'She's helping me in the investigation.'

'How do you do?' Joanna murmured. 'Please sit down.'

After they had seated themselves across the desk from her, the policewoman quietly took out a notebook and pencil, crossed her long legs neatly and sat poised to take notes. Joanna gave her a swift covert glance. A policewoman! Why would any woman, especially one as beautiful and well-groomed as this one, choose to work in such a dangerous, dirty profession?

'Now, Mrs Barnes,' Lieutenant Ryan began in a stiff, formal tone, 'I have a list here of all the hotel employees. I'd like to run through them with you now, if you don't mind, and get your opinion of each one. You do handle all the personnel problems, don't you?'

'Well, yes,' Joanna replied hesitantly, 'but I can tell you right now that there's nothing in the least suspicious about any of them. Mr Morgan and I both have complete confidence in every single person working here. In fact, most of them have been with the hotel for years.'

He sighed impatiently and gave her a stern look. 'I understand your reluctance to incriminate any of your people, but if you'll just bear with me, it will be a great help to my investigation.'

For the next two hours, he questioned her meticulously, going down the list of each employee, asking about their backgrounds, their habits, their personal lives. Joanna did her best, but she really didn't know much about their personal lives. She'd taken out the file on each one, but there was only strictly factual material in them, with no hint as to the character of the person involved.

Throughout the whole interview, Joanna would glance over from time to time at Laura Blake, who continued to sit calmly and silently by Stephen's side, her fingers flying efficiently as they spoke. Once or twice he would ask her if she'd caught a certain point he obviously thought was important, and the look that passed between them, at least on the blonde's part, looked to be far more than professional interest.

Finally it was over, and Stephen rose to his feet. 'I think that should do it for now,' he said. He turned to Laura Blake. 'I want you to interview the house-keeper, Mrs Murphy, now. I still have to question Mr Morgan's secretary.' He glanced at his watch. 'I'll meet you out in front in half an hour.'

'Yes, of course, Stephen,' she said, flashing him a far from professional smile. She closed up her notebook, and left the room, closing the door quietly behind her.

'I'm afraid I haven't been much help,' Joanna said, when the blonde was gone.

He gave her a quizzical look. 'You never know. Police work is largely a matter of painstaking detail. When all the facts are in, it's sometimes quite sur-prising how certain seemingly unimportant details come together to make a pattern and often give us the lead we're looking for.'

The last thing in the world Joanna was interested in was police procedure. The interview was over. She wanted him to leave so she could get on with her work. She rose to her feet.

'Well, if that's all——' she began.

'Not quite,' he interrupted. 'Actually, I wanted to ask you to have dinner with me one evening, perhaps this weekend.'

Joanna goggled at him, speechless. 'I beg your pardon?' she said when she found her voice.

He didn't say anything for several seconds. When he spoke again, there was a puzzled note in his voice. 'I asked you to have dinner with me.'

Well, she thought, do I want to have dinner with him or not? Was it really that simple? 'Are you al-lowed to fraternise with suspects?' she said, stalling for time.

'Ah, now you're only being obstructive,' he said smoothly. 'I already told you you're not a suspect.'

Something about the practised tone of his voice bothered her, even frightened her. There was just enough polished self-confidence in it, even a touch of arrogance, to make her realise that this was no ordinary man she was dealing with. She felt out of her depth, even in possible danger. Besides, the man was a policeman.

'Thank you,' she said stiffly. 'I'm sorry, I can't. I'm busy this weekend.'

'I'm sorry, too,' he said easily. 'Perhaps some other time.'

He turned from her and strolled nonchalantly out of the door and into the corridor. Joanna stared after him, her hands clenched into fists at her sides.

Of course, she thought, there was no question. She had to turn him down. She couldn't get involved with a policeman again, especially one as overbearing as this one. But why was it, then, she wondered, that she felt so let down?

# CHAPTER THREE

WITH Edward Morgan in the hospital, Joanna's duties seemed to triple, and she worked far into that night. She didn't even have time to go into Pensacola to visit him in the hospital as she'd planned, but since he'd given her express orders through Betty to stay at her post it was probably just as well.

The next morning, Martin Kingsley appeared at the door to her office. 'Hi, beautiful,' he called. 'I just stopped by to take a look at that letter you were so worried about.'

'Oh, good,' she replied, and started digging under the pile of papers on her desk. 'I'd forgotten all about it since Mr Morgan was hurt.' She finally found the letter and handed it to him. 'Have you seen him today?'

'Yes,' was the dry reply. 'He's turning the whole hospital upside-down, clamouring to be released.'

Joanna smiled. 'I can imagine that. I'm going to drive into Pensacola this evening to visit him.'

When he'd finished reading the letter, he bent down to slip it into the briefcase at his feet.

'Well,' she said anxiously, 'what do you think?'

'Just offhand, I'd say there's no case. I'll give the lawyer a call later today and let you know for sure, but I don't think you have anything to worry about.'

'That's a relief. Thanks, Martin.'

'My pleasure. That's what Edward pays me a retainer for.' He picked up the briefcase and rose to his feet. 'And now that that's settled, let's go have some lunch.'

Joanna frowned down at her cluttered desk. 'I don't know, Martin. I'm about to get buried under all this.'

'You have to eat,' he argued. 'Come on. I hate to eat alone.'

'All right,' she said. 'I guess I could use a little nourishment.'

They left her office and went down the hall together to the hotel coffee-shop, where they were seated at her usual table by the window. The sky was slightly over-hung with high wispy clouds today, casting a greyish film over the white sand and green water. The air was very still and heavy with humidity. Not a breath of a breeze ruffled the tall palm trees along the edge of the property line.

'Hurricane weather,' Martin remarked as they sat down.

'Don't say that!' Joanna said. 'I remember the last one, two years ago, and I can do without them quite well.'

'Oh, this building is solid enough to withstand anything.'

'I hope you're right.'

'I'm going to have a drink. Will you join me? It'll take your mind off the weather.'

She shook her head. 'No, thanks. I'm on duty, remember?'

'Then you need a drink; loosen up, and tell me all about the harrowing day you've had.'

'How do you know my day has been harrowing?' she asked.

'Aren't they all?'

'I suppose so,' she replied. 'And that's why I need a cool head.'

He gave her a disappointed look. 'Does that mean no drink?'

'Right. No drink.'

He sighed dramatically. 'Well, since I hate to drink alone, I guess I'll have to settle for food.' He went back to the menu.

Martin Kingsley had been a close friend of her husband and, as a lawyer, an enormous help to her in dealing with the intricacies of insurance, probate and inheritance taxes after his death.

'What are you doing in Miramar today?' she asked.

His fair head emerged once again and he gave her a hurt look. 'I came to see you, of course. I thought maybe if I asked you nicely one more time I might convince you to elope with me.'

Joanna laughed a little uncertainly. Although she was used to Martin's playful banter by now, she was never quite sure that underlying the light tone there wasn't a more serious intent than she was prepared to deal with.

She liked Martin. He had been a real support to her when Ross was killed, and later had been instrumental in finding the job for her at the hotel. But she wasn't really romantically interested in him or anyone else, and she dreaded the possibility that she would have to tell him so one day if he ever did press her seriously.

Just then his head swivelled around towards the window, and, following his gaze, she saw a luscious young bikini-clad blonde passing by on the path outside. She almost laughed aloud. There was hardly any fear of hurting Martin's feelings when his eye was so easily caught elsewhere.

When the blonde stepped off the path and started walking towards the beach, Martin turned back to

Joanna and gave her a sheepish look. Joanna eyed him sternly, heaved a sigh of mock resignation and shook her head slowly from side to side.

'I can't believe it, Martin,' she said sadly. 'The very second after you propose to me, your roving eye is caught by the first woman who comes along. It would never work.'

To her surprise, he flushed guiltily. 'Habit,' he muttered. 'Just habit.'

The waitress came to their table just then, and Joanna ordered her usual salad and iced tea. While Martin made up his mind what he wanted, she glanced over the crowded coffee-shop with a professional eye. Constantly on the alert for possible trouble spots or ways to improve the service in every area of the large hotel, she was, in effect, always on duty.

As she surveyed her domain, her eye suddenly fell on the tall figure of Stephen Ryan. She looked away quickly, hoping he hadn't noticed her, only to see Martin raise a hand beckoning him.

'Hello, Stephen,' he said, when the policeman arrived at their table. 'Won't you join us?'

The tall man nodded briefly at Joanna, and gave her an enquiring look. When she made no objection, he pulled out a vacant chair and sat down. 'Thanks,' he said. 'I will.'

Martin turned to Joanna. 'I suppose you already know that our stalwart policeman here is handling your robbery.'

'Yes,' she said stiffly. 'I know.'

During the short, strained silence that followed, Joanna gazed stonily out of the window at the Gulf. Stephen had apparently ordered his lunch on his way in, and after the waitress arrived with their meals the two men launched into a long involved discussion of the Miami Dolphins' chances for the Super Bowl this year.

While they ate, Joanna found herself making a swift mental comparison of the two men. The difference between them was remarkable. Martin was the perennial playboy, rarely serious, while the other man was withdrawn, remote, and had an air of quiet authority about him.

Martin downed his lunch quickly, and when he was through he rose to his feet, obviously anxious to get away. Joanna reflected wryly that the most potent reason for his hurry was probably still sunning herself down on the beach.

He shook hands with Stephen, and looked down at Joanna with a broad, teasing grin. 'Well, gorgeous, since I can't persuade you to run off with me today, I guess I'll be on my way.'

Joanna made a face at him. 'I'm going to take you up on that one of these days, Martin,' she warned. 'Just to see what happens.'

'I wish you would,' he said fervently.

She laughed. 'You'd run so fast, our heads would never stop spinning.'

He raised sandy eyebrows and waggled them. 'Just try me.'

When he was gone, she turned to find Stephen Ryan's gaze firmly fixed on her, his fork half-way to his mouth, a question in his startling blue eyes.

'Is that the reason you wouldn't go out to dinner with me?' he asked quietly with a nod at Martin's departing figure.

'No, it isn't,' she said without thinking.

'I see. It sounded serious.'

'If you know Martin at all, you should know he's never serious. Especially about women.'

He didn't say anything for some time, not until he'd finished his club sandwich and drained the last of his coffee. Then he settled back in his chair and gazed at her through half-closed, enquiring eyes.

'Well, then?' he said at last. 'What is your objection to me?'

Joanna was taken aback by the direct, unexpected question. 'I don't have to give you a reason.'

He shrugged and sat further back in his chair. 'I guess not.' He lifted his head and stared into space for a moment, then turned back to her and gave her a sudden broad smile. 'But it would be the polite thing to do, wouldn't it?'

That smile left her breathless. It transformed his hard features, and made him seem years younger. And much more attractive, too, she thought; quite handsome really, in a dark, saturnine way. She noticed for the first time that his dark hair was flecked here and there with grey, and she wondered how old he was. She dimly recalled Martin saying they'd been at school together, but that was before the robbery, and seemed like a lifetime ago.

'All right,' she said at last. 'Since you insist, my primary objection to you is that you're a policeman.'

His eyes narrowed. 'And why do you dislike policemen?'

'I don't dislike them,' she protested. 'I just made up my mind after Ross was killed that I'd never let one into my life again.'

He smiled again, more thinly this time. 'I'm not asking you to marry me,' he said, 'only out to dinner.'

She flushed deeply. 'I know that. It doesn't matter. I'd just rather not.'

He took a packet of cigarettes out of his shirt pocket and offered it to her. When she shook her head, he lit one of his own and slowly blew out smoke.

'I do seem to recall,' he said carefully, 'that you had a bad time of it after he was killed. Ross's death must have hit you very hard.'

'Yes,' she said tersely. 'It did.' He had to have heard all the gory details of her collapse. It had been common knowledge in the small, close-knit area.

'But you've come out of it all right. You seem very cool, very competent to me. Either you've recovered completely, or you put on a very good act.'

She had to smile. 'A little of both, maybe.'

'Then I'm surprised you've never married again,' he said in a conversational tone. 'Why not?'

Joanna was startled by the personal question. 'You're very direct,' she said tartly.

He nodded. 'It saves a lot of time.'

Then she laughed. 'You're one to talk. At least I have been married. Since you recommend it to me, why haven't you ever tried it yourself?'

He leaned forward across the table towards her. 'I wasn't exactly recommending it,' he said. 'And how do you know I've never been married?' Before she could think of an answer to that, he went on easily, 'But you're right. I'm a confirmed old bachelor. Like you, I don't think policemen make good husband material.'

He was not yet forty, she decided. Hadn't Martin said he was three years ahead of him in school? That would make him thirty-seven or thirty-eight. It was hard to tell, with the chameleon-like transformations in his appearance.

He stubbed out his cigarette in the ashtray on the table, then rose to his feet. 'I'll be on my way now.

I have to appear in court this afternoon. It was nice to see you again.' With a nod, he turned and walked away.

She stared after his retreating figure, tall and graceful as he threaded his way through the crowded room. As she watched him she had a moment's pang of regret that she hadn't taken him up on his dinner invitation. He was definitely a very attractive man, even an impressive one, with his broad shoulders, tall, straight carriage and dark good looks.

It wasn't until he had disappeared from view that it dawned on her that he hadn't asked her one question about the robbery.

That evening Joanna had an early supper alone, then decided to ride into Pensacola with Betty to visit Edward in the hospital.

It was just sunset when they set out from the hotel in Betty's Volkswagen. The morning's clouds had dispersed, and the air was balmy, the horizon suffused with a bright orange glow. There was very little traffic on the long straight road, but Betty seemed unusually silent and drove with fierce concentration.

Finally, when they had reached the outskirts of the small city and were stopped at a red light, Betty turned to her.

'Do you know what that old fool made me do?' she asked indignantly.

Joanna assumed she was speaking of Edward Morgan, and smiled. 'Well, no, I don't,' she said. 'What did he make you do?'

'He insisted I call Karen and ask her to come home.'

Joanna had never met Edward Morgan's prodigal daughter, but rumour had it that she had left Miramar, apparently under a cloud, some time before Joanna started working at the hotel. Her father never spoke of her.

The light changed just then, and with a great grinding of gears the small car lurched forward.

Hanging on to her seat-belt for dear life, Joanna asked, 'Do you think you can persuade her to come?'

Betty shrugged. 'I can try. I've called her several times, but can't get an answer, so I sent off a telegram this morning. It's up to her now. I tried to talk him out of it, but he only got mad and started yelling at me.'

'Well, he's a stubborn man.'

'Yes, but underneath he's badly shaken. I think that this scare has forced him to come to grips with his own mortality, even to the point where he wants to see that girl of his again.'

'Sounds as if Karen Morgan is not your favourite person,' Joanna commented lightly.

They were in front of the hospital now, and Betty pulled into a vacant parking space, shut off the engine, then turned and gave Joanna a direct look. 'You could say that. She was nothing but trouble as a girl, and if there's one thing Edward doesn't need right now, it's more trouble. I have no idea why he wants to see her after all these years. Sentimental old fool.'

When Joanna saw the glitter of tears in Betty's heavily mascaraed eyes, she wondered, and not for the first time, whether Edward Morgan and his faithful secretary had been involved in a relationship that was a great deal more than the casual friendship it appeared to be on the surface.

They went inside the hospital and made their way up the elevator and through the maze of medicinal-smelling corridors to Edward's room on the seventh floor. As they approached the room, voices could be heard coming from inside through the half-opened door. They stood there hesitantly for a moment, exchanging a glance. Then Betty shrugged, rapped smartly on the door and Joanna followed her into the room.

There was a white screen shielding the bed, and as Joanna stepped around it she came face to face with a grim-faced Stephen Ryan. She stopped dead in her tracks and stared at him.

He was standing at the foot of the bed looking down at an equally indignant Edward Morgan, whose head was still swathed in bandages. The two men were glaring at each other, and Joanna thought with some amusement that once again the indomitable policeman must have come up against her employer's stubborn refusal even to consider the possibility that any of his staff was involved in the robbery.

'Come on, Edward,' Stephen said then in a softer tone, 'if you won't co-operate with us, we can't very well protect you from future attacks, can we?'

Edward only grunted, and both men turned at the same time to glance at Betty and Joanna, acknowledging their presence with brief nods. The policeman looked down at Edward again, then began to walk away from the bed.

'I see you have visitors,' he said. 'I'll wait outside.' As he passed by Joanna, he gave her a cold look, and said, 'You're quite a pair. You must enjoy being robbed and shot.'

Joanna felt her hackles rise at his officious manner and met his stony gaze. 'You know, Lieutenant Ryan,' she said, 'we're not the criminals here. Aren't the police supposed to be on our side?'

They glared at each other across the bed, and for once Joanna was grateful for her height. It would be

so easy to be intimidated by this tall, stern man. There
wasn't a trace of softness in the hard features. Once
again, she noticed, he was impeccably dressed in a
dark suit, white shirt and tie. His lean cheeks and firm
jaw looked freshly shaven, and his crisp dark hair
recently cut.

He gave her one last scathing look, brushed past
her and stalked out of the room. When he was gone
she stepped over to the bed and put a hand on
Edward's good shoulder.

'How are you, Mr Morgan?' she said softly.

'I'm fine,' he said gruffly. 'Or I will be as soon as
I can get out of this place and the damned police leave
me alone.'

Betty had been standing on the other side of the
bed all this time, holding Edward's hand and gazing
down at him with undisguised concern. Now she
crossed her arms in front of her ample bosom and
snorted.

'Listen, Edward, the man is only doing his job. He's
right, you know. It could be an inside job.'

'Never,' Edward said firmly. 'My people are hand
picked. Most of them have been with me for years.
won't even discuss it.' He turned back to Joanna
'How are things at the hotel? Are you having any
problems?'

'Nothing I can't handle,' she replied. She told him
she had given the lawsuit letter to Martin to handle
then went on with a brief report on the running battle
between Mario and Ivan and how she intended to re
solve it, but he only seemed to be listening to her with
half an ear, and when she was finished he turned to
Betty.

'Have either you or Martin talked to Karen? Is she
coming?'

'I'm sorry, Edward,' Betty said. 'We're trying. We've both called her several times, but can't get an answer.'

'Well, I want you to keep trying. Call the police, send a telegram. Surely Martin can do something?'

There was a slight tremor in his voice, and Betty sat down on the edge of the bed, took his hands in hers and leaned over to smooth back the thinning grey hair.

'Edward,' she murmured soothingly, 'we *are* trying.'

Joanna coughed delicately. 'Er—I guess I'll wait outside for you, Betty,' she said, and when neither of them paid the slightest attention to her she turned and tiptoed quietly out of the room.

Stephen Ryan was standing in the corridor, leaning against the wall, his arms folded across his chest, glowering down at the floor. She went over to him and motioned with her head towards the closed door.

'Well,' she said, 'what's next? Thumbscrews and hot needles under the fingernails?'

He slowly pushed himself away from the wall and gave her a long, appraising look. 'I'm only doing my job,' he said quietly.

'Not a very nice one, is it?' she asked coldly.

He gave her a thin smile. 'No, I suppose not. But someone has to do it, and it's the one I've chosen.'

His mild manner made her feel ashamed of her tart comments, and she felt a sudden rush of sympathy for him. He *was* only doing his job, after all, and it couldn't be much fun for him to come up against one obstruction after another.

'I'm sorry,' she said, returning his smile. 'I haven't been the most co-operative witness, have I? My loyalties are rather divided, but I *am* on the side of right and justice.'

'That's understandable, and chances are this isn't an inside job at all. It's not a contest, after all. You and your boss seem to think we're on different sides. I just have to explore every avenue of approach, and this is a logical first step. You were married to a policeman. Surely you understand that?'

'I guess I did at one time,' she said slowly. 'But, as I mentioned before, I've tried to put everything about police work out of my mind. Too many unpleasant memories.'

'Well, I can't say I blame you,' he said quietly. 'It must be a hell of a burden for a woman to carry. You really hated it, didn't you, being married to a policeman?'

'No,' she said slowly. 'Ross and I were very happy together for the short time we were married. But——' She broke off.

Just then, Betty came out into the corridor. She stood in the doorway for a moment staring at them, then said, 'He's getting tired. We might as well go home, Joanna.' She turned to Stephen Ryan. 'I'm sorry he won't co-operate. He's a stubborn old man.'

'I'll give it one last try tonight,' he said, moving towards the door to Edward's room, 'then give it a rest for a while.'

They said goodnight, then, and Betty and Joanna went back down to the main floor and out to the car at the kerb. It was dark out, but the air was still soft and balmy, fresh and clean-smelling after the cloying hospital atmosphere.

They drove the short distance back to the hotel in silence for the most part, each woman wrapped in her own thoughts, but when Betty pulled off the main highway on to the narrow road that led towards the hotel car park she cleared her throat and gave Joanna a sideways glance.

'That's quite a man,' she said casually as she manoeuvred the car into her slot.

'Who? Mr Morgan?'

Betty snorted indignantly. 'No, of course not. I'm talking about Stephen.'

'Yes,' Joanna replied cautiously. 'I suppose so.'

'Interested in you, too.'

Joanna turned and stared at her. 'How can you tell that?'

Betty switched off the engine and started to open her door. 'Oh, the way he looked at you. I've been around a long time, kiddo. There's no mistaking that hungry look in a man's eyes.' She gave Joanna one quick backward glance and winked at her. 'Lucky you,' she said with a sigh, and got out on to the pavement.

For some reason, Joanna wasn't quite ready to let the subject drop just yet, and as they walked slowly together towards the brightly lit hotel she said, 'He did call and ask me to have dinner with him.'

'Good for you,' Betty said with feeling. 'When are you going?'

'I'm not. I turned him down.'

Betty stopped dead in her tracks and stared at her, under the light of a tall lamp-post. 'You turned him down?' Joanna nodded, and Betty shook her head. 'Why on earth did you do that?'

'I was married to a policeman, remember?' Joanna said with a lift of her chin. 'You can't imagine how awful it is to live in a constant state of apprehension over their safety. Sometimes I think that when it finally came, when Ross was actually killed, it was almost a relief. At least I didn't have to worry any more.'

They had started walking again, and Betty didn't say anything for a long time. When they reached the covered portico, Joanna started to step on to the path that led to her cottage, but Betty put a restraining hand on her arm.

'Is that your only objection to him? The danger of his job?'

'I guess so,' Joanna admitted.

Betty shook her head slowly from side to side and curled her lip. 'What if he had a nice, safe job?' she said. 'Say, something like owning a hotel. Like Edward.'

Bells started going off in Joanna's head, and she stared at Betty, speechless. Finally, she murmured haltingly, 'I never thought of that.'

Betty nodded vigorously. 'Sooner or later, my girl, you're going to have to come to terms with the fact that *life* is dangerous. There are no guarantees. What job could be safer than a semi-retired hotel owner? Yet Edward got badly hurt. Not killed, thank the lord, but he could have been.'

'You know, you're right,' Joanna said weakly. Then she shrugged. 'Although it doesn't matter. I made it pretty plain to him that I wasn't interested in getting involved with a policeman. He won't ask me again.'

'Don't be too sure. I don't think Stephen Ryan is the kind of man to give up easily.' She laughed. 'You saw how persistent he was with Edward, and I always thought *he* was the most stubborn man alive. Besides, you could always tell him you've changed your mind.'

'No,' Joanna said firmly. 'I couldn't do that.' Not after he was so cool and distant this evening, she added to herself. 'It's probably best to forget it, anyway.'

Betty raised one eyebrow and cocked her head to one side. 'I wonder if you'll find him that easy to forget,' she said, and with a little wave of her hand she pushed the glass door open and went inside the hotel.

Joanna stood looking after her for a few moments, then turned and walked slowly up the path towards her cottage. When she was inside she went straight to her desk, reached down in the bottom drawer, and took out the photograph album of wedding pictures.

As she slowly turned the pages, the smiling people all looked like strangers to her, as though they were enacting a drama that was now ancient history. Slowly she closed the book and replaced it in the drawer.

It was ancient history. The vow she'd taken when Ross was killed suddenly made no sense to her. Maybe Betty was right. Maybe she was being foolish to turn down the one man who'd seriously attracted her in the past three years. Perhaps it wasn't too late after all.

# CHAPTER FOUR

THE next morning was so hectic that all thoughts of her love-life had faded from Joanna's mind. The longer Edward Morgan was gone, the more keenly she felt his absence, even apart from the normal everyday problems that she had to cope with constantly.

Although he had given her full authority to run the hotel her way from the day she took over the manager's job, the knowledge that he was always there in the background to help her with major policy decisions had given her a sense of security she sorely missed now.

Her morning was mainly taken up in an attempt to resolve the raging hostilities between the Italian chef and the Russian *maître d'hôtel*. Both men were highly emotional, and had declared war the first day they'd met. If there wasn't a real problem that set them at each other's throats, she could count on them to invent one.

Today she called them both to her office and listened attentively to both sides of the current bone of contention between them, which hinged on Ivan's accusation that Mario deliberately delayed filling orders from the dining-room kitchen, so that the dinner guests blamed Ivan when their meals were served cold.

After listening to their impassioned recitations of grievances, real and imagined, for two solid hours, she had already made up her mind how to handle it.

When the last ugly word had been uttered, she rose from her desk, crossed her arms in front of her and gave first Ivan, then Mario, a long, penetrating look, just like a stern schoolteacher confronting two problem children.

When she spoke, her voice was clear and firm. 'You've both been here for two years now, and hardly a day has passed that there hasn't been trouble between you. I can't have that. It interferes with the smooth running of the hotel, which is my first responsibility. I don't know who's right and who's wrong here, and I don't care. I suspect there's a little of each. But if I hear one more complaint from either of you, I'll fire you both.'

They gazed at her, open-mouthed, for some moments, then glanced briefly at each other. Finally, with great dignity, Ivan rose to his feet and looked down his long Russian nose at her.

'You cannot fire me,' he pronounced. 'I quit.'

Then he turned and stalked out of her office. Mario, of course, was thrilled with this turn of events. He jumped up instantly from his chair and gave her a broad grin.

Joanna frowned at him. 'Before you start celebrating, Mario,' she said in a dry tone, 'you'd better consider the future. The next *maître d'* could be ten times worse than Ivan. In fact, if I were you, I'd try to make it up with him before he actually does leave. Who knows? I may hire a Frenchman next time.'

Mario gave her one horror-stricken look, then turned and dashed out of the room, fast on the heels of his old enemy. When he was gone, Joanna heaved a deep sigh and slumped back down in her chair. She had no idea how it would turn out, but she had serious doubts that Ivan would find a better job or that Mario

would prefer dealing with a fictional unknown
Frenchman.

She glanced at her watch. It was after one o'clock,
past her usual time for lunch. She called the coffee-
shop and had them send her a sandwich, and spent
her lunch hour going over the quarterly statement the
accountant had left with her yesterday.

That evening, after she'd locked up her office, she
looked for Betty to see if they could drive together to
the hospital to visit Edward Morgan, but when she
couldn't find her she decided to drive into Pensacola
by herself. She was still a little worried about how she
had handled the Mario-Ivan situation, and wanted to
discuss it with Edward in the hope he would corrob-
orate the action she had taken.

When she arrived at his room, Stephen Ryan was
just coming out. They both stopped short and stared
at each other for a moment, then he continued walking
towards her.

'I wouldn't go in there if I were you,' he said, and
a slow smile spread across the stern features.

'Why not?'

'Your redheaded friend and my star witness are now
going at it hammer and tongs.'

'And are you waiting to arrest one of them?'

He gave a harsh laugh. 'Hardly,' he said, and raised
one dark, quizzical eyebrow at her. 'Still determined
to cast me in the role of villain, I see.'

His good-natured acceptance of her barbed remark
made her feel suddenly ashamed of herself, and she
reddened. 'I apologise,' she said, then smiled at him,
raised a hand and held it stiffly in the air. 'I hereby
solemnly swear not to make any more obstructive
comments. Is that better?'

His smile broadened and he gazed at her appreciatively for several seconds. 'I'm just going off duty,' he said at last. 'I thought I'd get a bite to eat. Would you like to join me?'

All of a sudden, she knew she would, very much. What would be the harm? He was an attractive man. He was obviously interested in her. She had been positive he wouldn't ask her again, and the fact that he had said something about his ego. Either he was so self-confident that a rejection didn't bother him, or he was too arrogant to believe he'd been rejected in the first place.

'All right,' she said. 'I'd like that. It looks as though I won't be able to visit Edward tonight anyway. Maybe I'll just poke my head in for a minute and say hello.'

'I've got to call in,' he said. 'Give me five minutes and I'll drop back up here.'

She watched him walk away from her down the corridor in his long, confident stride until he disappeared around the corner to the bank of lifts. When he was gone, a sudden panic gripped her, and she turned quickly away. The simple dinner date somehow began to seem almost ominous. But Stephen Ryan meant her no harm. What was there to be frightened of? He'd said himself that he wasn't asking for a commitment, didn't even want one.

She opened the door to Edward's room and was immediately assaulted by the sound of voices raised in anger. She gave a few sharp knocks on the door to announce her presence, then stepped hesitantly inside.

Glancing from one angry face to the other, she said, 'Er—am I interrupting something important? If so, I can come back later. I just wanted to say hello.'

'Oh, no,' Betty said. 'Nothing important. Karen is coming, that's all.' It sounded as though the very words tasted foul.

'She's my daughter,' Edward growled from the bed.

'Some daughter,' Betty drawled with a curl of her glossy red lips.

'When is she coming?' Joanna asked.

'The loving prodigal is flying in tomorrow,' Betty replied sarcastically.

Joanna glanced at Edward. 'Well, I know you'll be glad to see her,' she said with a tentative smile.

Betty held up a hand and examined her long red nails minutely. 'For all the good it will do him,' she muttered.

Edward's face got red, then almost purple, and he opened his mouth. Before he could get out the first word, Joanna started backing towards the door. 'Well,' she said cheerfully, 'I'll be on my way. Glad to see you looking so well, Mr Morgan.'

Stephen was waiting for her out in the hall, and as they walked together down the corridor and into the waiting lift, Joanna's attack of nerves resurfaced. It had been a long time since she'd been out on a real date. What would they talk about? Would he get amorous later on?

'You know, Lieutenant Ryan,' she said in a light tone as the lift bore them downwards, 'you didn't have to buy me a dinner tonight to question me. You already know I'm a very law-abiding citizen and anxious to help the police any way I can.'

His eyes widened slightly, and he stared down at her. 'Stephen,' he said. 'My name is Stephen.' The blue gaze narrowed. 'That isn't why I asked you to have dinner with me. Why would you think that? If I'd wanted to question you again, I'd have said so.'

They had arrived at his car, a grey late-model Peugeot, and as she slid inside the spotless interior and settled back on the soft leather upholstery, she could smell the distinctive odour of newness and the faint, lingering aroma of tobacco.

'There's a good Italian restaurant out near the Naval Air Station,' he said on the way. 'How does that sound?'

'Great. I love Italian food.'

He drove silently and competently, in no particular hurry, but with the same concentration and poised energy he did everything else. It was clear to Joanna that he certainly felt no awkwardness about the situation, and she began to feel more at ease with him.

'Have you made any headway at all with your investigation of the robbery?' she asked.

They were stopped in a snarl of traffic, and he turned to her with a quizzical expression on his face, his dark eyebrows raised. 'Not much,' he said shortly, and turned his gaze back on the road ahead.

When the light finally changed, he shifted gears smoothly and inched the car forward into the left-turn lane. Joanna didn't pursue the subject of the robbery. His curt reply obviously meant he wasn't interested in talking shop when he was on his own time.

On the other hand, when they were parked in front of the restaurant and he shifted his position to ease his tall frame out of the car, she caught a brief glimpse of a holstered gun at his waist. Joanna was terrified of guns, and she shrank back in her seat at the sight of the ominous-looking leather holster. It brought it home to her once again that this man was involved in a very dangerous profession.

He gave her one sharp look, then crossed around in front of the car to open her door. When she got out, he took her lightly by the arm and they started walking towards the restaurant.

'One of the first things you should know about me,' he said casually when they reached the entrance, 'is that a policeman is always on duty.' He pushed open the door for her. 'But then, you do know that already, don't you?'

'Have you ever had to use it?' she asked faintly.

'Only when it was absolutely necessary,' he replied in a brusque, dismissive tone.

They stepped inside a crowded room with red checked cloths on the tables and a delicious tangy aroma in the air. Joanna hadn't had anything to eat since her light lunch, and she suddenly realised how hungry she was.

By the time their dinner was served, her earlier nervousness was forgotten. Stephen had a relaxed manner about him that made even his silences comfortable, and she found his detached air of reserve quite pleasant, even challenging. This distance made her curious about him. She thought again about the gun and his curt replies to her questions about his work.

'Do you like being a policeman?' she asked.

'Yes. Very much.'

'Did you always want to be one?'

He had finished his cannelloni by now, and after the waitress brought their coffee he sat back comfortably in his chair and lit a cigarette.

'No, not at first.'

'A fireman?'

He shook his head and smiled. 'Worse. A lawyer.'

She perked up her ears, and the wheels began to turn in her head. 'That's interesting. My father is a lawyer. He has a small practice in a suburb on the outskirts of Boston.'

'Successful?' he asked.

'Successful enough to need more help,' she replied. 'He'd like to take it easier, and I think he's probably already looking for someone to take into his practice.'

She eyed him carefully, but he didn't show any great interest in the subject. He only nodded and continued to smoke in silence.

'What made you change your mind about the law?' she asked.

'Several things,' he replied promptly. 'After I finished law school I practised for a few years at a big firm in Miami, but eventually decided I'd rather put the bad guys behind bars than defend them. The law pays much better than police work, of course, but at some point I made up my mind that money wasn't everything anyway.'

'Why did you decide to come back to the Gulf Coast?'

'Mainly because of my parents. They were quite elderly, and when my father had a stroke my mother was barely able to care for him. I was an only child— one of those midlife surprises—and I just decided it was up to me to do what I could for them.'

'It must have been hard for you, though,' she murmured, 'to leave the big city, the better career opportunities.'

'Not really. I was already becoming disenchanted with the law by then anyway, as well as city life.' He leaned forward, his elbows on the table. 'How about you? Do you like hotel management?'

'Oh, I love it. It's very satisfying work. Even though some of the personnel problems can get a little hairy.' She told him about her problems with Mario and Ivan.

'And how did you handle it?' he asked, amused. 'Did you rap their knuckles? Stand them in a corner?'

She laughed. 'Not quite. They're both bigger than I am.'

'I don't imagine you're a pushover, though,' he said, eyeing her speculatively.

'Oh, no. I can be quite firm when I have to.'

'I know,' he said with feeling. He hesitated for a moment, then added, 'You've come a long way from that frightened little girl of three years ago.'

His voice was light, but there was an undertone of approval in it that warmed her. 'Yes. I guess I have,' she said.

The young Italian waitress appeared just then to ask if they wanted an after-dinner drink. She was an attractive brunette, small and rather buxom, wearing a low-cut peasant costume, and Joanna watched, half amused, half annoyed, as she leaned over to speak to Stephen with a wide, inviting smile. Stephen ordered a brandy and gave Joanna an enquiring glance.

'I think I'll stick with coffee,' she said.

She excused herself then to go to the powder-room, and as she repaired her make-up in front of the brightly lit mirror she suddenly noticed the bright gleam in her hazel eyes and the pleased half-smile on her face.

She was actually enjoying herself! It was really quite pleasant to be sought after by such an attractive man. And a policeman at that! Yet he didn't seem to want to talk about his work. He'd shut her off abruptly when she'd asked him about the robbery. It was just as well.

She snapped her bag shut and went back into the dining-room. When she caught her first glimpse of him sitting there, quite still, his back towards her, gazing out of the window, she stopped for a second to look at him.

Even though all she could see was the back of his dark head and the wide shoulders in the dark suit, a pleasant warmth, a little stirring of incipient desire, stirred within her. He was so blatantly *male*! And surely he himself must be aware of how appealing he was to women? How could he miss it, considering the way the cocktail waitress had encouraged him to investigate her pronounced cleavage?

When she sat down across from him, he nodded at the cup of steaming coffee at her place. 'You're sure you won't have a drink?'

'No, thanks. The coffee is very good here.'

He didn't say anything for a few moments, but she was aware of his frankly appraising gaze. 'Tell me about yourself, Joanna,' he said at last. 'Is there an important relationship in your life?'

'Not at the moment,' she murmured. She took a sip of coffee.

'But surely you've come close to marrying again after all these years since Ross died?'

She gave him a direct look over the rim of her cup. 'That depends on what you mean by "coming close". But I would have to say no.'

'No romances? No grand passions? I can hardly believe that.'

'Well, you'll just have to take my word for it. I've been too busy. I haven't had the time.'

'Ah, a liberated woman.'

Joanna frowned. 'I don't like labels like that. I've had to take care of myself, and I've done it. Besides, I really do love my work. And as far as I'm concerned, all women's lib has done is given men the licence to behave even more irresponsibly than they did before.'

He spluttered at that, half choking on his brandy. 'You don't have a very high opinion of men.'

She shrugged. 'They're only people, as weak and fallible in their way as women. I don't dislike men. I'm not a man-hater, if that's what you mean, and I've never felt in the least oppressed by them.' She grinned. 'In fact, some of my best friends are men.'

'But you've decided you can live without us.'

'As far as allowing one to dominate my life, yes.'

'Well, Joanna, we'll see about that.' He rose to his feet. 'Are you ready to leave?'

They drove back to the hospital in silence. The traffic was quite heavy, and Stephen gave all his attention to the road. Joanna gave him an occasional sideways glance as he drove. His profile was outlined against the bright lights along the street, and his fine features were set in a look of total concentration. His large, capable hands rested on the steering wheel in a relaxed confident grip, and as he shifted the gears his movements were controlled and graceful.

It wasn't until he pulled into the hospital car park and she directed him to where she had left her car that she began to worry again. What exactly would he expect from her now? Everything? She had a sudden attack of shyness. Married at twenty-two, and rigidly celibate ever since her husband died, she'd had very little experience in these matters.

When he switched off the engine and pulled on the hand-brake, she looked at him. 'Thank you very much, Stephen,' she said stiffly, 'for the wonderful dinner.'

'Thank you, Joanna,' he said, 'for the pleasant company. I'll see you to your car.'

The hospital grounds were almost deserted by now, and as they walked slowly together across the car park, not touching, not speaking, Joanna listened to their footsteps echoing hollowly on the pavement, and re-alised they were quite alone. She fumbled in her handbag for her keys, and by the time they reached the small Datsun her heart was pounding with nervous anticipation.

She unlocked the door, pulled it open slightly and turned to him to say goodnight. The bright moonlight overhead cast interesting shadows on his lean face, and she caught her breath as he reached out a hand and touched the shining dark hair that fell loosely around her face.

'You have beautiful hair,' he murmured. 'Like a blackbird's wings. I like the way you wear it, too.'

He placed his hand lightly on her cheek and leaned down towards her. At his touch, a slow heat began to build in her. He had been so formal during the evening. Now the warm, caressing fingers, moving over her cheeks, her forehead, her mouth, stirred a sudden strange, shuddering longing in her.

She closed her eyes and waited, wondering if he was going to kiss her, knowing she wanted him to, even that she wanted more, much more, afraid she was already in over her head. Stephen continued merely to explore the contours of her face, and by now she was rigid with suspense. Finally one hand came to rest under her chin, and he tilted her head slowly upward.

His lips pressed first against her forehead, then brushed lightly over her cheeks to the corner of her mouth, until they finally settled against hers. His mouth was warm and mobile, and the practised restraint with which he held back from deepening the kiss only made her long for more.

Every muscle in her body seemed to go slack as his hands moved to her shoulders and began to knead them gently. There was no hint of threat in his warm touch, and although their bodies were lightly pressed together the embrace was almost chaste.

Then, suddenly, he withdrew from her. Startled, she opened her eyes to see one last fleeting smile on his face before his hands dropped from her shoulders. He reached down, pulled open the door to her car and held it for her.

'Goodnight, Joanna,' he said.

Numbly, she got inside and inserted the key in the ignition. When the engine caught, he turned and walked off towards the grey Peugeot, and as she drove the short distance back to Miramar she couldn't make up her mind whether to feel insulted or relieved at the abrupt way he had left her. If she didn't appeal to him, why would he ask her out? Perhaps he was just being considerate.

If only he didn't have such a dangerous job! She'd been disappointed when he hadn't picked up on the mention of her father's need for help in his law practice. Perhaps in time, if their relationship progressed, she might bring it up again. It would solve everything.

Later, as she stood in front of her mirror in her nightgown brushing her hair, she gazed at her reflection. Like a blackbird's wings, he'd said. That was really quite poetic, especially for a policeman. But then, he was not like any other policeman she'd ever known. She put her fingers to her mouth where his lips had pressed so softly against her own, and a great surge of longing rose up in her, almost frightening in its intensity.

No one had ever made her feel quite this way before, not even Ross, and she was shocked by his ability to carry her into the world of passion this way. Tonight she had been ready to follow him anywhere he wanted to take her. A man with that kind of power over her could be dangerous.

The next day Joanna managed to get away from her desk long enough to dash into the coffee-shop for a quick lunch. Martin Kingsley was there at her table, beckoning to her.

'I just wanted to tell you your worries are over about that lawsuit,' he said.

'Wonderful,' she breathed, sitting down. 'How did you manage that?'

'I called the lawyer and we agreed there was really no case in law. He was just humouring an old client.'

'Well, that's a load off my mind. Now, if you could just solve all my personnel problems, I'd——'

She broke off abruptly when she saw Stephen Ryan walking towards their table. At the sight of him, her heart gave one swift leap, then settled down into its normal rhythm as she watched him approach. He looked wonderful, she thought, freshly shaven, his dark hair combed neatly and wearing one of his conservative dark suits, crisp white shirt and muted tie.

Then she heard Martin give a low whistle. 'Wow,' he said with feeling. 'Will you look at what old Stephen has unearthed?'

It was then that she noticed the blonde at Stephen's side. She was very young, surely not more than twenty-two or twenty-three, perhaps even younger, and very beautiful. They made quite a handsome couple, as a

matter of fact, and the sight of them together sent a
sudden sharp stab of jealousy through her.

She turned around quickly to see that Martin was
goggling openly, his mouth hanging open, almost
slavering. She felt like slapping him. Fat lot of good
he'd do her.

She sat quite still, turning her water glass around
and around on the table, wishing she could vanish
into thin air. A few seconds later she heard Stephen's
voice behind her, and turned around slowly to look
up at him. His expression was unreadable.

'Joanna,' he said in his stiffest formal tone, 'this
is Edward Morgan's daughter, Karen. Karen, Joanna
Barnes, the manager of the hotel. You probably
already know Martin Kingsley.'

Martin had leaped to his feet at their approach and
pulled out a chair. He was now standing beside it,
grinning foolishly at Karen. 'Practically from the
cradle,' he said. 'How are you, Karen? It's been a
long time.'

The girl murmured a polite 'How do you do?' to
Joanna, then turned to Martin and flashed him an
arch, knowing smile. 'Hello, Martin. It's good to see
you again.'

She seated herself gracefully, and while Martin
made a big show of pushing in her chair Joanna took
a closer look at the girl. She really was lovely, she
thought, one of those pale, willowy blondes, fragile
as a Dresden doll, rather tall, and dressed in a well-
fitting, very flattering black dress that did nothing to
hide her near-perfect figure. Her long blonde hair
hung in a shimmering veil around her delicate features, flowing down in graceful waves to her shoulders,
and she wore just a trace of pale make-up, artfully
applied.

'Well, Karen,' Martin was saying heartily, 'so you decided to come, after all. Your father will be pleased.' He darted a glance at Stephen. 'Although I don't know why you needed a police escort. I was planning to pick you up later at the airport myself.'

'Karen caught an earlier flight,' Stephen said easily. He looked at Joanna. 'I was at the hospital with Edward when she called. Since I was in Pensacola anyway, he asked me to meet her plane. And here we are,' he ended up lamely.

Of course, Joanna thought, they would know each other, coming from the same small town. She turned to the girl. 'I want you to know how concerned we've all been about your father's injuries, although he does seem to be mending nicely. Please let me know if there's anything I can do for you while you're here.'

Karen flashed her a dimpled smile. 'Thank you very much, Mrs Barnes,' she said in a rather childish voice.

Joanna winced inwardly at the respectful tone. It sounded just like a little girl being polite to her elders and made her feel positively ancient. 'Joanna, please,' she said.

Karen gave her another distant smile, as though humouring her, then turned to an apparently mesmerised Martin and focused all her attention on him.

With a little shrug, Joanna turned to Stephen, who was seated next to her. 'How are you this morning, Stephen?' she asked in a stiff, polite tone.

He gave her a tight, narrow-eyed look. 'It really was a coincidence,' he muttered almost inaudibly.

Joanna raised her eyebrows and flashed a pleasant smile at him. 'It doesn't matter in the slightest,' she lied. She glanced at Karen, then back at Stephen. 'She's a very lovely girl.'

Before he could reply, Karen broke in. 'Stephen,' she said in an imperious tone, 'I'm really not at all hungry right now. I couldn't eat a thing.'

Joanna pushed her chair back and stood up. 'Of course,' she said quietly, 'you must be tired after your trip and will want to get settled. I'll show you to your father's apartment now if you like. Mrs Murphy can get the extra bedroom ready for you later, but you probably want to freshen up now after your trip.'

Karen gazed up at her out of wide blue eyes and blinked once. 'Oh, don't bother,' she said. 'I know where it is.' She turned to Stephen and put a hand on his arm. 'Will you come with me, Stephen?' she pleaded helplessly. Then, when he hesitated, 'Pretty please?'

Stephen looked at Joanna, an enigmatic expression on his lean face, then rose to his feet. 'Of course,' he said. 'Joanna, do you have the key?'

'You can pick it up from Andy at the desk,' Joanna said, sinking back down in her chair.

Stephen nodded, pulled out Karen's chair, and took her by the arm to help her up. She flashed him a grateful, adoring look, then leaned heavily against him and gazed down at Joanna.

'I'm so happy to have met you—er—Joanna,' she said sweetly. 'And I'm sorry to be so much trouble.' She waved a well-manicured hand helplessly in the air. 'But I'm sure you'll understand.'

'Of course,' Joanna murmured. 'And let me know if you need anything.'

'Right,' Martin echoed heartily. 'That goes for me, too.'

They left then, and Martin's eyes followed them every step of the way as they walked through the crowded restaurant towards the entrance. When they were gone, he turned back to Joanna, his broad, good-looking face spread with a fatuous grin.

'Well!' he said with feeling.

'Well, what?' she asked, forcing out a smile.

He shrugged. 'What can I say?' He leaned back in his chair and lit a cigarette. 'It looks as though the famous Karen Morgan has come home to stay,' he said at last, breathing out smoke.

'Famous?' Joanna asked. 'What do you mean by that?'

Martin propped his elbows on the table and leaned towards her, his eyebrows raised in a knowing look. 'Surely you've heard the story of how she left Miramar?'

'Well, no, as a matter of fact I haven't,' she replied. She eyed him carefully. 'I didn't realise you'd known her that well when she was living here.'

'I didn't, really. We only met a few times. But I knew *of* her. Remember, I was living in Pensacola before you and Ross arrived, and at that time the name of Karen Morgan was already legend along the whole Gulf Coast of Florida, probably Alabama and Louisiana, as well.'

Joanna's eyes widened and she stared at him. 'You must be mistaken,' she said. 'Why, that was over five years ago. She couldn't have been more than sixteen or seventeen.'

He nodded cheerfully. 'I'd say that's about right.' He gave her a puzzled look. 'What does age have to do with it?'

Joanna was hopelessly confused by this time. 'Well, I don't know. Nothing, I suppose.' She thought a minute. 'Why did she leave Miramar? Did Edward make her go?'

'Oh, no, he doted on her. That was probably half her trouble. Apparently he spoiled her rotten, and eventually just couldn't handle her. Just ask Betty,' he added with a grin.

Joanna had to smile. 'Yes, I've already heard her version.'

'The story is,' Martin went on, 'that she ran off with a musician, Tony something or other, who played in one of the bars in Panama City, and when Edward found out about the affair he put his foot down, told her she couldn't see him any more. But it was too late, way, way too late by then.'

'So she married him?'

Martin shrugged. 'Who knows? There was a rumour of a child, but as far as I know that's the last anyone ever heard from her or of her again.'

'Yet she did come back to be with her father when he asked her to. You'll have to give her credit for that.'

'We'll see.' He stubbed out his cigarette and shook his head at her. 'Sometimes I worry about you, Joanna. You're always so determined to see the best in everyone, you're bound to be disappointed, even taken advantage of.'

'I resent that,' she said heatedly. 'You make me sound like some empty-headed, naïve Pollyanna. My life hasn't been *that* sheltered, after all.' She eyed him carefully. 'Besides, I didn't notice you putting up much resistance to her charms. You were falling all over yourself to get her attention.'

He only shrugged and gave her a wicked grin. 'Well, since you won't give me a tumble, what am I supposed to do? Become a crusty old bachelor like Stephen?' Then he sobered. 'Did it ever occur to you that with Edward temporarily out of the picture, the lovely Karen may have come back to Miramar to take over the hotel?'

Joanna stared at him. 'The thought never entered my head,' she replied slowly. 'She's never shown any interest in Miramar in the past. Why would she suddenly develop a desire to run it now?'

'Maybe you should think about it,' he went on in an unusually grave tone. 'If Karen Morgan is anything like her reputation, you can bet she has something up her sleeve by coming back to Miramar at all. Somehow I don't think it was entirely filial duty.'

'Well, right now I don't have time to worry about that, Martin,' she said with a smile. 'Besides,' she continued, raising an eyebrow at him, 'in spite of your suspicious nature, you're obviously not entirely immune to Karen's charms yourself. Not that I blame you. She's a beautiful girl.'

'Oh, I'm not. She's a luscious morsel, all right.' He eyed her maliciously. 'Better watch out, Joanna. She's got Stephen eating out of her hand already.'

She suppressed the urge to smack the knowing grin off his face, well aware that he was only baiting her, and instead she only returned his smile.

'That's Stephen's lookout, isn't it?' she said composedly. 'I have enough on my plate at the moment trying to keep the hotel running with Edward gone, without having to worry about Stephen.' Then, sobering at the reminder, she added, 'I can't tell you how much I miss him. I'm not sure I can manage without him much longer.'

'Oh, you'll manage just fine,' Martin said cheerfully. 'That's just your style, to gird up your loins and charge into battle in a crisis.'

She made a face at him, took a last swallow of coffee and rose to her feet. 'Speaking of which, duty calls. I'll see you later.'

# CHAPTER FIVE

IT WAS Joanna's day to inspect the kitchens of the coffee-shop and dining-room, and go over the week's menus with the chefs. She got to it right after lunch, and it was after three o'clock that afternoon by the time she got back to her office. The telephone was ringing as she unlocked the door, and she hurried over to her desk to answer it.

'This is Mrs Barnes. May I help you?'

'Joanna? It's Stephen.'

At the sound of his voice, her heart started to race and she sank slowly down into her chair. 'Hello, Stephen.'

'Listen, I wanted to explain to you about Karen.'

'There's no need to do that, Stephen. Besides, you already did this lunchtime.'

'I was afraid you might get the wrong idea,' he went on. 'It was strictly a favour for Edward Morgan.'

Joanna breathed a deep inner sigh of relief. 'Well, thank you for calling to explain, but it really wasn't necessary.'

'All right. Just so long as you understand that there's not now, nor ever has been, any love lost in that quarter.' He hesitated, then said, 'Would you like to take in a movie on Saturday? I noticed that one of my favourites is playing at a cinema in Panama City. *Raiders of the Lost Ark*. Have you seen it?'

'No, I haven't,' she said, stalling for time.

Did she want to go? She didn't at all like the way she'd felt that lunchtime when he'd shown up with

Karen Morgan in tow. She'd never been jealous before in her life, and if that was what was in store for her if she embarked on any kind of relationship with this man, it might be wiser to call a halt to it before it became seriously important to her.

He was speaking again. 'I don't know how lofty your literary standards are, but I found it extremely entertaining and amusing. How about it, then? We could have an early dinner before the show.'

Well, she thought, throwing caution to the winds, yes, she did want to go. 'All right,' she said. 'It sounds like fun.'

'Good. I'll pick you up around six.'

After they had hung up, Joanna leaned her elbows on the top of her desk, rested her chin in her hands and sat there staring into space for a long time, a pleased little smile on her face, her fears forgotten. He wasn't interested in the lovely Karen. He did want to see her again.


The cinema was located in a district of Panama City that resembled a miniature Greenwich village, with fine restaurants next to shabby taverns, an art gallery connected to a used clothing store, record shops, musicians playing on street corners and every conceivable variation in between.

The pavements were crowded on Saturday night, with a cross-section of society to be seen milling about. It was spring vacation, and groups of students from the nearby college congregated on street corners; wide-eyed families from the neighbouring states strolled along, looking out of place; gorgeous young men dressed in tight jeans swished by arm in arm, chattering volubly; and there was a large contingent of ageing, still stoned hippies left over from the seventies standing around in a daze.

The smell of marijuana was heavy on the balmy spring air, and loud music blared from the open doorways of several dimly lit establishments, where seedy, disreputable-looking characters hung around the entrances.

It was not a place where a woman would feel comfortable alone after dark, and Joanna was glad of Stephen's tall, reassuring presence as they walked the two blocks from the restaurant to the cinema. When they crossed the street he held her lightly but firmly by the elbow, and his quiet, confident manner made her feel quite safe, even cherished.

Since it was to be an informal evening, and a little cool, she had worn low-heeled shoes with her plaid pleated skirt and red sweater, and he seemed much taller to her this evening, a deeply satisfying phenomenon to a woman who stood five feet nine in her stocking feet.

He also looked quite different in his casual clothes—well-fitting tan chinos, a white shirt open at the throat, and a soft, sable-coloured corduroy jacket with leather patches at the elbows—and, if anything, even more attractive.

At the cinema, Stephen bought the tickets and they walked inside the foyer. The wall directly in front of them was covered with a large mirror. As they approached it, Joanna's glance was caught by their reflections, and she thought with some surprise that they made quite a handsome couple.

Stephen's head was bent as he shoved change into his wallet, and, as he replaced it in the hip pocket of his trousers, once again she caught a glimpse of the wicked-looking revolver holster at his belt. She shuddered a little at the sight and started to look away, but he raised his head just then and their eyes met in the mirror.

As though able to read her thoughts, he held her gaze in his for a second, smiled briefly at her, then took her arm again and gave it a slight reassuring squeeze.

'Do you smell that?' he asked, with a lift of his head.

She turned to him, sniffing the air, which was filled with the delicious scent of hot buttered popcorn. He raised an enquiring eyebrow.

'Guilty!' she said with a smile. 'I love it.'

'Can you eat a whole box yourself, or shall we share?'

'I'd like my own, please,' she said without hesitation. 'I'm very selfish when it comes to popcorn.'

He nodded. 'Good. A woman after my own heart.'

The movie was as wonderful as he had promised, full of action, adventure and romance, fast-paced, with never a dull moment and, in spots, hilarious. Joanna couldn't take her eyes off the screen, so intent on one exciting scene after another that she finished her box of popcorn without even realising it.

There was a pleasant feeling of intimacy in the darkened cinema, and a slow warmth that generated between them so gradually that Joanna only became aware of it when she felt their hands clasp together during the exciting chase sequence.

It was the first time they had really touched that evening. His grip was firm, his fingers long, the palm calloused. She glanced covertly at him, not moving her head, and her heart caught in her throat at the sight of his clean, strong profile.

He was slouched down slightly in his seat, one elbow resting on the wooden arm, his long legs spread apart in front of him. He seemed to be totally absorbed in the action on the screen, yet she knew he too must feel the tension, the warmth between them. It was almost palpable in the close air.

Then, during the love scene, that tension heightened and imperceptibly she felt him easing her arm closer against his body until it was tucked securely under his, and she knew he did feel it, too. It wasn't all in her mind.

At the end of the film, the lights went on and he turned to her. They were sitting so close together now that his piercing blue eyes seemed scarcely an inch away, and she could see the fine lines around them, the slight dark stubble on his lean cheeks and firm jaw, and smell the clean fragrance of his skin.

'Did you enjoy the movie?' he asked in a low voice.

She smiled. 'Very much. I can understand why you wanted to see it again.'

'Shall we go, then?'

She nodded, and they got up and started edging their way to the crowded aisle, where everyone seemed to be leaving at once. As they inched their way towards the exit through the steady stream of people, he put both hands on her shoulders, and the long body pressed up against hers created a burning sensation along her spine that grew stronger with each step she took.

Outside on the pavement the night air had grown chilly, and as they walked along he kept one arm around her shoulders, drawing her slightly up against him.

They chatted for a while about the movie on their way back to Miramar, but eventually the topic was exhausted, and he seemed to withdraw from her, driving in silence, while she sat straight in her seat, some distance away from him, her hands clasped in her lap, wondering what was coming, what he would expect from her.

He had pulled off the main highway now and parked in front of her cottage. Without a word, he shut off the engine and turned to her. She could only stare at him, trapped in the steady blue gaze like an animal caught in the glare of a car's oncoming headlights.

She opened her mouth to speak, but before she could get the first word out he had jumped out of the car and come around to open her door. He took her by the hand, and they walked slowly up the path towards the cottage.

She took out her key and unlocked the door, uncertain whether to invite him in or wait until he asked. She turned and looked up at him, hoping to find an answer in his face, but all she saw was his typically serious, rather remote expression. His dark eyebrows were slightly raised, as though he, too, was asking a question.

Something in that grave look reassured her, made her believe that, whatever it was he wanted from her, he meant her no harm.

She smiled up at him. 'Thank you, Stephen, for a wonderful evening. I really did enjoy the movie immensely.'

'I'm glad,' he said.

They were silent for a few moments, gazing into each other's eyes. In just another second, she thought, the silence was going to become awkward. Clearly, he was leaving the next move up to her.

Then she made up her mind. 'Would you like a drink?'

'Yes, thank you,' he said with a nod. 'I would.'

'Come inside, then,' she said, unlocking the door and switching on the hall light.

When the door was shut behind them and she had led the way into the living-room, the awkwardness returned. 'Sit down,' she said, indicating the couch. 'I'll just be a minute. Is Scotch all right for you?'

He was standing in the middle of the living-room, very much at ease, his hands in his trouser-pocket, jingling keys, his sharp blue eyes taking in every detail of the small room. His head turned slowly towards her.

'Yes, Scotch would be fine. With soda, if you have it. If not, water will do.'

Definitely a man who knew his own mind, she thought. 'I'll just be a minute, then. Make yourself at home.'

Alone in the kitchen, she had another attack of nerves. Her heart began to thud painfully, and she could hardly keep her hands steady as she poured the Scotch.

She wished she'd had more experience with this kind of thing, but even she didn't live in a cave. You couldn't spend one day working in a hotel without quickly grasping the fact that most young people, even teenagers, hopped in and out of bed like rabbits.

Stephen Ryan was a mature, self-assured man who probably had his pick of desirable women. Yet he seemed to be attracted to her. She certainly felt a strong attraction for *him*, and the warmth she'd experienced in the cinema had to be mutual.

When she came back, hanging tightly on to the tray of drinks so she wouldn't drop it, he seemed to have taken her at her word and made himself at home. He was sitting on the couch, leaning forward, his legs apart, his elbows braced on his knees, leafing through the collection of magazines on the coffee-table in front of him.

He looked up at her, then rose to his feet. When he took the tray from her, his hand brushed against hers, and her pulse-rate started to escalate again.

'You like gardening, I see,' he commented with a nod at the ferns and begonias and African violets that clustered in front of the north window. 'You'll have to come to my house and give me some advice one of these days.'

Her first swallow of Scotch had calmed her down a little, and she sat down beside him. 'What kind of plants do you have?' she asked.

He laughed. 'One very sick rubber plant that someone gave me a few years ago. It needs help badly. I think it has a fatal disease of some kind—or is trying to commit suicide.'

'Well, I'm not really an expert. I do admit to carrying on conversations with my plants, however. I don't know how much good it does them, as the experts claim, but I enjoy it.'

He drained his drink, then set the glass down and turned to her. For a moment she thought he was going to get up and leave, but he sat quite still with his eyes firmly fastened on her. Joanna began to feel uneasy under the steady blue gaze.

'Is something wrong?' she asked.

'Not at all. I just keep wondering why a beautiful woman like you has cut herself off from romance. Or were you fibbing when you told me that?'

'No,' she said, 'I was telling you the truth. Why would I lie about a thing like that?' She laughed nervously and took another swallow of her Scotch. 'Actually, Ross has been the only man in my life.'

He gave her a blank look. 'You're kidding.'

Now, why did I tell him that? she groaned inwardly. She could feel her face reddening under his steady gaze, and turned her head away, staring miserably down at the floor.

'You must have loved him very much,' he said softly.

She raised her head again and looked at him. 'I suppose I did. It's been so long ago, though, and we were so young when we married that sometimes I even have trouble remembering what he looked like.'

'Then you're not still grieving for him,' he said carefully.

She thought for a minute, then said, 'No, I don't think so. I do think, however, that I still resent the way he was taken from me. It hurt a lot at the time.'

'Well, Joanna,' he said, setting his drink down on the coffee table and turning to her, 'I'd like to make you forget that hurt.'

She held her breath, waiting, unable to tear her eyes from him, and when he reached out his hands to place them on her shoulders her heart rose up in her throat. He bent his head down slowly towards her, and she closed her eyes as his lips pressed against hers, gently, softly, tentatively at first, as though testing her reaction.

She sank towards him, her mouth softening under his. His arms came around her, and the kiss deepened as he pulled her up against him. He was holding her tightly to him now, all along the length of his hard, muscular body, and his mobile mouth pulled sensuously on hers, opening now and drawing in her parted lips, as one large hand moved slowly up and down over her back.

Joanna felt as though she was drowning. It had been so long that she had forgotten what it felt like to be held in a man's arms, to be crushed against a strong chest, the rasp of a male stubble on her cheek, the clean, masculine scent of his skin and hair all around her.

Her mind went blank and sheer instinct took over. Greedily she raised her arms up around him to run her fingers over the smooth skin at the back of his neck, up into his thick dark hair, underneath his loose shirt collar, and when his hand came around to settle on her breast, the warm, strong touch aroused an intensity of emotion in her so powerful that it brought tears to her eyes.

He raised his head to gaze down into her eyes. 'I want you, Joanna,' he said huskily.

Somehow, hearing the words revived all her old caution, and she sensed that she was getting in over her head, that soon she would be lost and have to give him whatever he asked of her. She stared at him wordlessly, and what she saw in that steady blue gaze frightened her. Was she really ready for this? She felt herself to be on the edge of a precipice, in real danger of plunging over the side. She opened her mouth to speak, but no words came.

As he watched her, his mouth quirked up in a rueful smile. 'But it's too soon, isn't it?' he asked gently.

Dumbly, she nodded. He gave her a quick kiss on the mouth and released her. 'Then I think I'd better get out of here.' He rose abruptly to his feet. 'Don't get up,' he said. 'I'll let myself out.' He reached down to touch her hair. 'I'll call you.'

The next thing she knew, he was gone. She heard the front door close firmly behind him, and as she sat there, still dazed, her hand over her mouth, listening to him drive away, the house seemed suddenly very cold and empty. Even though her head told her it was better that he left when he did, in her heart she had wanted him to stay. Fighting back a dull ache of disappointment, she got up and walked slowly down the hall to her bedroom.

From then on, Joanna's world suddenly seemed to be full of Stephen Ryan. For the next two weeks they saw each other almost every day. He would appear at the door to her office around noon and they would eat lunch together in the coffee-shop. On her visits to the hospital to see Edward Morgan, Stephen was invariably there, and they fell into the habit of going out for dinner afterwards.

Throughout all this time his lovemaking remained restrained but, as the days passed, the tension building up between them began to take its toll. When he held her stiffly in his arms for his goodnight kiss, she knew it was costing him an enormous effort to hold back. She herself longed for more, but didn't know how to tell him so.

Each time he left her she felt more and more bereft. A touch of his hand on her bare arm, his lips moving slowly over hers, his long, hard body pressed against her, all set up a heated response she was finding it harder and harder to deny.

As she came to know him better, his habit of mind, his reactions to everyday events, his very body language, she became aware of the warmth that lay beneath the reserved exterior and began to realise that what she had once seen as coldness was actually a protective mechanism, built up bit by bit through his years as a policeman, someone whose entire working life consisted of dealing with crime, violence, even death.

He never discussed his work with her, however, and whenever she broached the subject he seemed to tense and draw back from her mentally. Then he would smile and change the subject. Eventually she stopped speaking of it at all, and managed at last to lull herself into the illusion that the danger didn't exist.

Finally, on a Monday morning, Edward Morgan was released from the hospital, his wounds all healed. Martin had driven Karen, Edward's daughter, into Pensacola to pick him up, and while they were gone Joanna assembled the whole staff in the lobby to form a reception for his homecoming.

Betty and Mrs Murphy had constructed a large 'Welcome Home' banner out of coloured paper, and Andy had helped them hang it over the entrance. Everyone had pitched in to make it a memorable occasion, and even Mario and Ivan had again buried the hatchet, this time in honour of their employer's return.

When they arrived, Martin got out of the car and came around to open the back door, obviously intending to help Edward out, but when Edward stepped out on the pavement he shook Martin's hand off his arm with a gesture of impatience. Then he simply stood there, his sharp eyes moving first up at the colourful banner, then down at his assembled staff. The expression on his face changed from sheer amazement to a broad grin of delight, and then his features settled into a stern mask.

'Welcome home, Mr Morgan,' Joanna said as she went forward to greet him.

'Bunch of damned nonsense,' he growled with a nod at the decorations.

When she saw the glitter of tears in his eyes, Joanna had to smile. 'Well, it pleased them to do it for you,' she said, taking his arm. 'We've all missed you.'

They made their way in a little procession into the lobby and through the crowd of well-wishers, which included several of the hotel's older guests, people who had been coming to Miramar for years and wanted to join in the festivities.

'All right, all right,' Edward said gruffly as he acknowledged the hearty greetings on his way. 'That's enough of that. Get back to work now, all of you.'

Joanna and Martin were standing together by the front desk, and he gave her a knowing look. 'Don't believe a word of it,' he said with a grin. 'He loves the attention, but would never admit it in a million years.'

'It's so good to have him back,' Joanna said, returning his smile. 'I felt lost without him.'

'Seems to me you did all right on your own.' Then he frowned and lowered his voice. 'But I feel I should warn you. He and Karen had quite an interesting conversation on the drive home from the hospital. It seems she's decided to stay on indefinitely. She's got some idea in her head that she wants to learn the hotel business, and of course her doting papa is thrilled.'

'Well, I guess that's only natural,' Joanna said slowly.

The news disturbed her a little, but she dismissed the tiny prick of concern instantly. It was her father's hotel, after all, and he had a right to do whatever he wanted with it, make anyone he pleased the general manager. He'd never offered her an ironbound contract, and if Karen did take over her job there were other hotels in the world. The experience she'd gained at the Miramar would be invaluable in finding another position.

'Learning the hotel business isn't something that happens overnight,' she added, 'so I don't imagine my job is in any immediate danger.'

'Not if Edward has any sense,' Martin said stoutly. 'Just don't be surprised if she starts interfering with your work.'

'I take my orders from Edward Morgan,' Joanna replied. 'If one of them is to teach his daughter how to run a hotel, then that's what I'll do.'

They were walking down the hall toward Edward's office now, trailing behind him as he limped along, Karen at his side. A beaming Betty was at the door waiting to greet him, her red hair blazing, her fresh make-up piled on lavishly. She immediately started to make a fuss over him, and he responded with indignant noises of protest.

As he and Betty disappeared into his office, Karen turned around and came walking towards Joanna. 'Oh, Joanna,' she said, 'Daddy and I had a little talk on the way home from the hospital, and he wants me to start helping you as a sort of assistant. I hope you don't mind. If I'm going to stay in Miramar I'll really need something to do.'

Joanna glanced at the blonde girl, deeply tanned now from almost three weeks of doing absolutely nothing but sunning herself on the beach, painting her toenails and entertaining herself with Martin Kingsley.

'Of course I don't mind,' Joanna replied in a pleasant tone. Then she added, 'If that's what your father wants.'

The girl's face clouded over momentarily, then she brightened. 'By the way,' she said smoothly, 'have you heard? The police have caught the men who robbed the hotel and injured Daddy.'

Joanna darted a quick glance at Martin. 'Really? When did that happen?'

Martin opened his mouth to speak, but Karen was already rushing on. 'Stephen mentioned it last night at dinner. We're all so pleased that none of the hotel staff was involved.' With a sweet smile, she turned and followed her father and Betty into his office.

Speechless at that bit of news, Joanna stood there staring after her. Last night she'd been too busy with the preparations for Edward's homecoming party to visit him at the hospital, so she hadn't seen Stephen. And he'd had dinner with Karen!

Yet he had told her there was nothing between them. Had he lied to her? Turning away from Martin to hide her burning cheeks, she started to go into her own office, but he put a restraining hand on her arm, holding her back.

'Er—listen, Joanna,' he said in a hesitant tone. 'Don't pay any attention to anything Karen says. She hasn't changed. She still thinks she's got to get her hooks into every man who comes along. The fact that you've been seeing Stephen only whets her appetite.'

'Don't worry about it, Martin,' she said, striving hard for a light tone. 'You make it sound more serious than it really is.' She smiled at him. 'I don't own Stephen Ryan, after all. Now, I really should get to work. With the boss back, I have to be on my toes.' Especially, she added to herself glumly, if his daughter is after my job, as well as my man.

'Will you please listen to me?' he said. 'It's nothing like she's trying to make it out to be. Stephen came to the hospital early last evening especially to tell Edward they'd caught the men who'd beaten him and that no one from the hotel was involved. Since Edward was ready to be released today anyway, his doctor let him out on a pass, and we all had dinner down in the cafeteria. That's all there was to it.'

At his words, the world began to look a little brighter, but she didn't want him to see that. 'Thanks, Martin,' she said. 'It's still none of my business, though, and doesn't really matter.'

But it did matter, she thought as she went into her office. It mattered more than she'd ever dreamed it would. She closed the door, then went over and sat down at her desk. What she had felt when Karen had made her announcement was nothing less than an intense blast of blind, possessive fury. She shook her head. What was happening to her? Was she already hopelessly in love with him?

What cruel fate was it that forced her into these irresistible attractions for men who courted danger? First Ross, now Stephen.

'My destiny,' she groaned aloud, and buried her face in her hands.

Joanna didn't hear from Stephen at all for the next few days, and hardly a moment passed when she didn't wonder why. Did he think her too prudish? Was he tired of having to rein in his perfectly normal desires out of consideration for her? Desires the lovely Karen would probably be only too happy to satisfy.

Now that the robbery was solved, he probably wouldn't even be coming to the hotel any more, either. She tried to put the nagging thoughts of him out of her mind, telling herself she didn't want to get involved with a policeman again anyway, but she knew she was lying. She simply didn't care about that any more, not since she'd known Stephen.

The simple truth was that she missed him terribly. She kept imagining she saw him during those long days, his dark head, his tall, straight carriage, and each time the telephone rang she snatched it up eagerly, praying it would be him.

She had just about given up hope that she'd ever even see him again when he finally did call. It was a week after Edward had come home, on a Tuesday night, and she was in her cottage, reading on the couch in the living-room, when the telephone rang. At the sound of his deep voice her heart turned over once, then settled down to a steady beat.

'Joanna,' he said. 'It's Stephen.'

'Hello, Stephen,' she said calmly.

'I would have called sooner,' he went on, 'but I've had night duty for the past week, and since you work during the day there wasn't much hope of our getting together.'

'Well, it's nice to hear from you again. How have you been?'

'Good. I called to see if you felt up to sampling some bachelor cooking this weekend,' he continued matter-of-factly.

'What did you have in mind?' she asked, keeping it light.

'I'd like to show you my house, for one thing.'

She hesitated, wondering if that was such a good idea. Yet she didn't want to turn him down.

'I didn't know you could cook,' she teased.

'I can't,' he replied promptly. 'But I keep a good supply of bicarbonate on hand. How does Saturday sound? It'll be my first weekend off in a long time, and I'd like to celebrate.'

'That sounds fine.'

'Good. Shall I pick you up around five o'clock?'

'Oh, there's no need for that. Give me the directions and I'll find my own way.'

Saturday, she thought, after they'd hung up. She would see Stephen again on Saturday, only four more days.

Wednesday was Joanna's day off, and she drove into Panama City to do some shopping. Her father's birthday was coming up in a few weeks, and he was such a difficult man to buy for that she wanted to look for his gift early and get it in the mail in plenty of time.

It was a lovely spring day in late May, the azaleas were blooming, the sun shining, and while she strolled along the pleasant mall she decided on an impulse to buy a new dress. She wanted to look pretty for Stephen on Saturday, and her entire wardrobe seemed to consist of nothing but conservative business wear.

In the mall there was a wonderful little boutique where she'd bought clothes in the past. A flattering colour this time, she thought firmly as she entered the small shop. Nothing violent and nothing provocative. Just a good, sensible dress that she could wear to other functions.

The middle-aged, gushing saleswoman set Joanna's teeth on edge with her 'honey's and 'dear's, but she did seem to know a lot about clothes. 'No bright colours for you, dearie,' she said decisively, gazing at Joanna with a critical eye. 'With your dark hair and pale complexion, you can wear just about any pastel. Maybe a light blue or a nice soft shade of green.'

Joanna stood there dressed only in her slip, almost suffocating in the tiny dressing-room. She hated trying on clothes, and after rejecting three dresses that did absolutely nothing for her she decided that one of her old skirt suits with a pretty blouse would have to do.

Just as she was reaching for her own clothes, the saleswoman poked her head inside with another dress over her arm. 'Try this on, honey,' she said. 'I think it's just what you're looking for.'

Joanna sighed and allowed the woman to help her on with the dress, promising herself that this was absolutely the last one. When it was zipped up the back, she turned to look in the full-length mirror on the wall of the dressing-room.

It was perfect, she thought, a pale apricot shade that looked good enough to eat. The material was a fine polished cotton, very springy, and cut in such a way that even with her rather sturdy bone-structure she looked positively sylphlike. The round neckline was low enough to show off her creamy throat and upper chest, but not blatantly suggestive.

'I'll take it,' she said.

'You've made a wise choice, dear,' the saleswoman said. 'Will that be cash or charge card?'

# CHAPTER SIX

STEPHEN'S house was an astonishing revelation to Joanna. He lived about half-way between Miramar and Pensacola on an isolated spit of land that jutted out into a small bay.

The house itself was unpretentious, even a little rustic, and surrounded by tall palm trees and weeping cypress trees. There were two bedrooms, a bath, and one large all-purpose room that was dominated by a huge stone fireplace. The floor was planked oak with colourful rugs scattered about. It was obviously a man's house, with shabby worn leather furniture and no sign of a soft, feminine touch.

Stephen had set up a redwood picnic table in the back where a shaggy lawn sloped down to the waterfront. A brick barbecue was built in one corner of the flagstone terrace, and after a thorough tour of the house Joanna sat on a chaise-longue in the sun while he prepared the coals for the fire.

His back was towards her, his posture relaxed and casual as he worked over the fire, and she could watch him to her heart's content without his being aware of it. He was dressed in a pair of worn, low-slung jeans and a blue knitted shirt, and looked even more wonderful in these casual clothes than in his habitual suit and tie.

'There,' he said, turning to her. 'That should do it for now. Half an hour for the coals to catch, then I can put the steaks on.'

He walked across the terrace towards her in his easy, relaxed gait and sat down on the chaise next to her. There was a low redwood table between them upon which their drinks were set. He took his glass and raised it.

'It's a little early for gin and tonic. If you'd prefer something else, I can probably oblige.'

'No, thanks,' she said, taking a sip of the tart, sour drink. 'This is fine.'

He leaned back in the chaise. 'Well,' he said. 'What do you think?'

'About your house?' she asked. 'All this?' She waved a hand to encompass the whole lovely scene of lawn, trees and blue water. 'It's beautiful, Stephen. I envy you.'

He nodded diffidently. 'I've been lucky. The property was left to me by my parents, along with just enough of the wherewithal to pay the taxes and a bit left over. It's why I was able to give up practising law and go into police work.'

She took a sip of her drink and smiled at him. 'Why did you become a lawyer if you didn't like it?'

'I didn't know I wouldn't like it until I tried it, for one thing.' He shook his head. 'Why does anyone choose one line of work over another? My father was a lawyer, and I think to begin with I probably just drifted into it to please him, but as time went on I found I liked it less and less, especially the cut-throat competition among lawyers, at least in the big city firms.'

'Have you ever thought of going back to it?' she asked carefully.

He shook his head. 'Not for a minute. Life is too short to spend it clawing your way to the top. Someone always gets hurt, and when you get there, what have you got?' He waved a hand to encompass the beautiful property that surrounded them. 'Having this, plus work I enjoy and am good at—that's more important to me than what the world calls success.'

'But police work has its own problems, doesn't it?'

He shrugged. 'It's a risky business, and, I'll have to admit, sometimes a sordid one, but aside from the fact that I like it, it's also a very necessary one.'

There was a short silence then. The sun was lowering in the western sky, casting shadows through the leafy cypress trees, and there was a low hum of insects in the background.

Finally, she turned to him. 'Karen told me you'd arrested the men who robbed the hotel.'

'That's right.'

'When was that?'

He took a long swallow of his drink and looked away. 'A few weeks ago. Two weeks ago last Thursday, as a matter of fact.'

She thought for a moment. 'Then you knew about it before we went to the movies that Saturday night. Why didn't you mention it to me then?'

'I don't know. It didn't seem important.' He hesitated for a moment, then said, 'That's not true. I didn't tell you because I was afraid it would upset you to be reminded of my work, what I do.'

He reached for the pack of cigarettes lying on the table and lit one. Was she upset? she wondered, watching him. No, she decided, she wasn't. It all seemed very remote to her now in the peaceful setting. Several sail-boats skimmed along the surface of the bay in the late afternoon breeze, and the noisy engine of a power-boat could be heard nearby.

'But I'm over all that,' she said finally. 'I think I have been for a long time and just didn't realise it.

As terrible as it was to lose Ross that way, what really
did me in was my own immaturity. I'd counted on
Ross to be there for me, the way my father always
was, telling me what to do, how to live, what to think,
and it was terrifying to suddenly be on my own like
that for the first time in my life.'

He gazed at her intently. 'Yes, I imagine it was.'

'I was so young when Ross and I married, barely
twenty-two, and I'd never really been independent
before, so that when he was killed I just went to
pieces.' She reached out and put a hand on his arm.
'But I *am* over it, Stephen,' she added softly.

He didn't say anything, but the taut muscles of his
arm relaxed imperceptibly, the lines on his forehead
smoothed out, and the pleased look on his face told
her all she needed to know.

After a moment he downed the last of his drink,
rose to his feet and stood smiling down at her. 'The
coals should be just about perfect by now. I'll get the
rest of our dinner.'

He crossed over to the barbecue, and after he put
the steaks on the hot grill he disappeared into the
house.

When he was gone, Joanna sat up and finished the
last of her drink. She was filled with a deep contentment. It wasn't just his physical appeal, she
thought, as he came strolling back outside balancing
a large tray filled with food and crockery. That was
powerful enough, but it was the man himself, the way
he had protected her from all reminders of his
dangerous work, as though he really cared about her
feelings.

A real prize, she thought, rising to her feet and
clearing the table so he could set the tray down.

'Steaks are done to a turn,' he called to her from the barbecue. 'Come and get it.'

It was dark by the time they finished dinner. Joanna helped carry things into the small kitchen alcove and offered to help clean up.

'Never mind about that,' he said. 'I have a wonderful woman who comes in to take care of me for a few hours once a week. Let's go in the other room. It's getting chilly, and I've got a fire laid.'

She followed him into the large main room which, although handsomely proportioned, still conveyed an air of intimacy through the casual groupings of furniture. There was a couch and a low table in front of the stone fireplace. Joanna sat down to watch him while he lit the kindling.

'Do you like music?' he asked.

'Yes, I do, although I don't know much about it.' She laughed. 'You know how it goes—"I know what I like,"' she quoted, '"but I don't know why I like it."'

'Well, there's plenty to choose from,' he said with a nod at a stereo set in one corner of the room. 'Pick out something you like.'

She chose an album of old show tunes from a large collection that included everything from modern jazz to the classics, and set it on the turntable. 'You're going to have to come and push the proper buttons,' she called to him. 'These complex systems terrify me.'

He strolled over to her side, got the turntable spinning, and the room was suddenly filled with music.

'Come and sit down,' he said. He took her by the hand and led her over to the crackling fire.

When they were seated side by side on the couch, he kept her hand in his. He leaned his head back, closed his eyes and sighed contentedly. There was only one dim lamp burning on the far side of the room, and as Joanna gazed over at him, the firelight flickering over his fine, strong features, she was filled with a deep sense of contentment.

He opened his eyes and smiled at her. 'It's been a good day, Joanna,' he said in a low voice.

She nodded. 'Yes, Stephen. It has.'

'I missed you this past week,' he went on. 'I almost called you several times. But I needed some time to think.' He hesitated, then smiled. 'Besides, I was getting a little tired of all those cold showers.'

Her eyes flew open. 'Stephen! Are you serious?'

'No, not literally. But I've had a hell of a time keeping my hands off you lately. Surely you know that?'

'Yes,' she admitted. 'Of course I do.'

His hand tightened on hers then, drawing her slowly towards him. There was no forcing, no abrupt pull, only a slight but inexorable pressure that she had no will to resist. Her eyes never left that commanding blue gaze until his arms came around her. Then she closed them with a sigh.

As he drew her into his strong embrace, his lips pressed against her eyelids, her forehead, light, feathery kisses that burned her skin wherever they touched it. His hand was at her throat now, pushing her head back, his long fingers moving along her jawline in a firm stroking motion.

His mouth came down on hers at last, softly, gently, at first, then with a more demanding pressure. There was real urgency in his kiss now. His mouth opened wider, and she could feel his tongue seeking entry, forcing her own lips apart.

All her senses were aroused—the wonderful male scent of tobacco and the fresh outdoors, the feel of his hand on her skin, the faint taste of the liquor he had drunk, the sound of his breath in her ear. Her lips parted and she strained towards him eagerly, clutching at him, melting against him. Then, with his open mouth still claiming hers, he pressed her backwards on the couch and the hand at her throat slid downwards to cover her breast.

He lifted his head and gazed down at her. One dark lock had fallen to curve over his forehead, and the blue eyes were glazed with desire. As the hand on her breast began to move slowly back and forth in a slow, sensuous caress, his glance flicked down to watch the steady rise and fall of her heaving chest.

She lay there, breathing shallowly, staring up at him, when suddenly he pulled back from her and reached down to raise her up beside him. He laced his fingers through hers in a firm grip, then turned to face the fire, scowling into the flames as though deep in thought. Bewildered by his abrupt withdrawal, Joanna watched him, waiting for him to speak.

When he finally turned to face her again, his expression was sober, even slightly troubled. 'I've got some leave coming,' he began slowly. 'I can take it any time. I thought I'd go down to the Florida Keys, do some fishing, a little sailing. A friend of mine owns a small hotel at Key Largo and runs a charter boat.'

It was the last thing she had expected. 'When will you be leaving?' she asked carefully.

'That depends.'

'On what?'

'On you.' He held her eyes in his. 'I want you to go with me, Joanna.'

She stiffened and drew in a sharp breath. 'You mean...'

He nodded gravely. 'I want you, Joanna,' he said in a husky voice. 'And I think you want me, too.'

'Yes,' she whispered. 'But——'

He put a finger on her lips. 'I like you a lot,' he said. 'I also know quite well that you're not the kind of woman to hop in bed with every man who comes along. You're a very special person, and the last thing in the world I want is to harm you in any way.' He smiled crookedly and rubbed his thumb over her mouth. 'But I do want you. Badly.'

Joanna's mind raced as she considered the implications of his unexpected invitation. Of course she wanted him, and a week alone with him sounded like heaven to her. But was she ready for this? Did he really expect her to go off with him just like that? He was moving too fast for her.

'But before you decide whether you want to go with me,' he went on in a low steady tone, 'I think it's only fair to you to be totally up front about my feelings. I want you to know that I think you're everything a woman should be.' He drew in a deep breath. 'In fact, I'm already half in love with you, and I believe we could have a fine, really special relationship.'

But—Joanna said to herself. She knew there was going to be a 'but' to end his speech. She could see it coming and steeled herself. What could it be? Was he married? Engaged?

'I never wanted a permanent tie,' he went on. 'I never saw any possibility, ever, of my wanting to marry or settle down. I told you once that I didn't think policemen made good husband material. I've seen one marriage after another, one serious relationship after another fail among my co-workers because eventually their wives or sweethearts were unable to tolerate the danger their men were in. Your own experience only confirms that conviction.'

Actually, she had stopped listening to him right after the part about his not wanting a permanent tie. All the softness was gone from his face, and the cold, remote expression of the policeman was back. It would be futile to argue with him now.

She raised herself up, moved away from him and gave him a cool look. 'You don't give me much credit, do you, Stephen?'

In the lamplight she could see him scowl darkly, but before he could say anything she went on hurriedly, 'You claim you're worried about my reaction to your work, but then you also admit you don't want a permanent tie anyway. Perhaps what you really mean is that you want to go to bed with me, but without a commitment of any kind. I can't do that. I've told you a hundred times I'm over my fears, but I need some assurance that you care about me.'

He drew back from her, then rose to his feet and walked over to the fireplace. He stood for some time with his back to her, gazing down into the fire, then came back to sit down beside her, a solemn, intense look on his face.

'I do care,' he said in a low, earnest tone. 'It's *because* I care that I'm telling you that a committed relationship with a policeman has dangers that even you might not be aware of.' He ran a hand over his dark hair. 'I'm afraid you'd end up like so many others, walking out on me the first time I got hurt, or you had to sit at home knowing I was out on a dangerous assignment.'

'I think you've got to let me be the judge of that, Stephen. Don't treat me like a child. You have no right to make that kind of decision for me.'

He looked away from her and stared blankly into the fire, his hands clasped between his knees. She waited several moments for him to speak, but when he remained silent she rose abruptly to her feet, smoothing down the skirt of the apricot dress.

'I think I want to leave now,' she said, moving towards the door. 'Don't come with me. I can find my own way out.'

He was on his feet in a flash, striding after her. 'Joanna, don't go,' he called. When she kept on, he put a hand on her arm and forced her around bodily to face him. 'What's wrong?' he said. 'I didn't mean——'

'What you meant, Stephen,' she bit out, 'is perfectly clear. To you I'm just a way to fill in the emptiness in your life, a temporary distraction.'

'That's not true,' he growled. 'And you know it. Do you think I ask just anybody to go away with me like that? Do you have any idea how long it's been since——?' He broke off and dropped his hands from her arms. 'Give me credit for some discrimination, Joanna. If I didn't care about you I wouldn't have bothered to ask.'

'It doesn't matter, Stephen. I could never tolerate an affair. Not with you, not with anyone else. I'm just not built that way. I care about you, too, you know, and I think it will be better all around to break it off now before it gets more involved.'

'Well, then,' he said angrily, 'will you please tell me what it is you do want? I'm not a mind reader, you know.'

'I want some assurance that there's at least a chance we might be heading somewhere. I don't want a brief fling, a trip to the Keys and then a goodbye.'

'It wouldn't be like that!' he shouted.

She put her hands on her hips and glared at him. 'Well, just how would it be, Stephen?'

He looked away, rubbing a hand along his jaw, and staring unhappily down at the floor. 'I don't know,' he mumbled at last. He turned to her. 'I just don't know.'

She sighed. It was exactly what she'd been afraid of. 'I'd better go,' she said softly. 'Goodnight, Stephen.'

As she walked away from him, she prayed silently that he would call her back. But he remained silent. When she reached the door, she opened it slowly, let herself out, then closed it quietly behind her and quickened her step down the path.

Driving home through the dark, she kept her eyes fixed straight ahead, firmly resisting any regrets. It could never work his way, and it was better to end it now, before committing herself physically to him. Then it would be impossible. She'd just have to forget him.

During the next few days, however, she found this wasn't quite so easy to do. Her wayward thoughts strayed constantly to the tall man with the piercing blue eyes who had found his way into her heart just when she least expected it. He had breached her defences so thoroughly that life without him now seemed cold and empty.

As she tossed and turned in her bed at night, or sat at her desk staring into space during the day, she wondered how she ever could have imagined she had been content with her life before Stephen came along. The empty years alone now seemed like a barren desert, and what lay ahead of her without him a vast, trackless waste.

She looked for him everywhere, jumped every time the telephone rang, and had to strain her will-power to the breaking point to keep from calling him and telling him she had been wrong, that anything was better than life without him, that she wanted him on any terms.

Finally, by noon on Wednesday, she couldn't stand it another minute, and with a pounding heart and shaky fingers she dialled his office number.

'Pensacola Police Department,' came a woman's voice. 'Laura Blake speaking.'

Joanna's throat constricted when she heard the name. It was the good-looking policewoman who had been with Stephen that day he'd questioned her about the robbery. She cleared her throat nervously.

'May I speak to Stephen Ryan, please?' she said.

'I'm sorry. Lieutenant Ryan is on leave this week. Can someone else help you?'

'No. No, thank you. I needed to speak to him personally.'

'May I take a message, then?'

There was just a shade of irritation in the woman's tone, and Joanna wondered if she recognised her voice. She hadn't given her name, had she? She was so nervous by now that her palms were damp and the telephone kept sliding in her hand.

'No message,' she said at last. 'I'll catch him when he comes back.'

They hung up then. So he *had* taken his leave. And she could have been with him if she hadn't been so stiff-necked and proud. She groaned aloud at the chance she had missed. Now she'd never see him again. Tears smarted behind her eyes and she swallowed convulsively, choking them back. There would be plenty of time for tears later.

The next day Joanna awoke to a heavy, overcast sky. The weather seemed to mirror her own depressed state of mind, and she stared gloomily out of the window at the grey sky. It was her day off, and after showering and picking at a meagre breakfast of toast and coffee she puttered listlessly around the cottage all day, getting nothing at all accomplished.

Finally, by late afternoon, still restless, she decided a walk on the beach in the fresh air might revive her heavy spirits. The morning's clouds had gradually dispersed to reveal patches of blue sky, but a cool breeze was still blowing off the Gulf. She threw a sweater over her lightweight cotton dress, locked the door to her cottage and went outside.

Just as she started down the path from her cottage to the beach, she heard someone call her name. When she turned around to see Stephen walking briskly towards her, her heart flipped over at the mere sight of him. She stopped short and waited, her whole body rigid with suspense, until finally he stood before her.

She looked up at him. 'Stephen,' was all she could say.

His face was grey and drawn beneath the heavy tan, and the little lines at the corners of his eyes were more deeply etched. He stood gazing down at her, a look of abject misery clouding his face, his eyes boring into hers.

Joanna's heart was pounding so heavily that she was sure he could hear it, even above the steady roar of the surf. He didn't say anything. He just stared hungrily into her eyes as though the very sight of her was food for a starving man.

'I—I thought you were away,' she finally faltered.

'I was,' he said shortly. 'I came back.'

'I see.' A dim ray of hope seized her. Maybe it wasn't too late. 'Why?'

'I couldn't stay away,' he replied. Then his mouth twisted into a wry smile. 'You've cast a spell on me.' As he searched her face, the smile slowly faded, and his expression grew grave. 'Joanna, I've got to talk to you.'

'All right. I was just going to take a walk on the beach.'

'Do you mind if I walk with you?'

'No, of course not.'

He took her by the arm, and they started walking down towards the beach, strolling along in silence all the way up to the far end of the Miramar property, a good hundred yards. At the end of it a small thicket of palm trees and oleander marked the boundary, and they sat down on one of the wooden benches placed there by the hotel for the convenience of the guests.

He sat for a long time, his long legs spread apart, his elbows resting on his knees, leaning forward and staring out at the sea. It was very quiet, with only the rolling of the tide, the birds calling to each other overhead and the gentle swaying of the tall palm trees to break the stillness.

Finally he turned to her. 'I was alone down there, in Key Largo,' he said. 'And I had a lot of time to think.' He paused for a moment, and she waited breathlessly. 'I want you to know that I was wrong. I should have realised that you weren't the kind of woman to enter into a casual affair. I should never have suggested it. But please try to understand. I've always believed it was a mistake for policemen to marry, and with your history it seemed disastrous.'

She couldn't remain silent any longer. 'But I already told you——' she started to protest.

'I know. And I want to believe you.' He raised a hand to her face and smoothed the heavy dark hair back from her forehead. 'I had a hell of a time during the past week to keep from calling you, you know. But every time I picked up the telephone I thought about the look on your face the first time you saw my gun.'

She wanted to stop him. How could she convince him that she really had conquered the old fears? But her instinct told her to keep quiet and let him talk.

'What worries me,' he went on, 'is that even though you think it won't bother you now, when a real test comes along, it might turn out to be more than you can handle.'

Her spirits sank. Nothing had changed. 'I don't know what more I can say to convince you, Stephen,' she said at last. 'It's up to you. You either believe me and trust that I mean what I say, or you don't.'

He rose to his feet and turned from her, staring out over the water, his hands in the back pockets of his jeans. The sun had just sunk below the horizon, and the grey clouds were forming again. Soon it would be dark.

Finally he turned back to her and reached for her hand, raising her up to stand before him. Drawing her into his arms, he buried his face in her hair.

'I do care about you, Joanna, and I want it to work between us. I guess if you're willing to try, I am too.'

She looked up into his eyes, the piercing blue shining brightly even in the gathering dusk, penetrating to her very heart. She knew then just how much she had come to want him, to need him, to love him. He lowered his lips to hers in a long, sweet, gentle kiss that filled her with warmth and reassurance.

When the first drops began to spatter down on them, he looked up at the sky. 'It's going to pour soon. Shall we go back to your place? We still have some talking to do.'

With his arm around her shoulders, they ran back down the beach to her cottage and arrived there just before the skies opened up and the heavy rain began. The minute they were inside, the door closed behind them, he drew her into his arms and they clung together wordlessly for several moments.

As the insistent heat began to build between them, she raised her arms up around his neck, pressing herself against the hard-muscled chest, raking her fingers through his hair, drinking in the clean scent of him. When his mouth moved to cover hers she melted towards him, and they kissed deeply, hungrily, like drowning people clinging to a raft.

He finally tore his mouth from hers and gazed down at her, the blue eyes blazing. 'I don't know what's ahead of us,' he said gravely. 'But I want you to know that I do care about you. I'll never lie to you, and I'll never wilfully harm you in any way.'

She believed him absolutely. 'I know,' she murmured.

He rubbed his thumb over her mouth, his eyes never leaving hers. 'There's something else I think we should discuss before we go any further,' he said in a solemn tone.

Joanna smiled at him. 'That sounds ominous.'

He shook his head. 'No, not at all.' He led her over to the couch in the living-room, and when they were seated side by side he turned to her.

'First of all,' he began, 'I want to assure you again that I haven't the slightest interest in Karen Morgan.' He took her hands in his. 'However, I'm thirty-eight years old, and you already know I'm not at all monklike in temperament or habits.'

'I do know that,' she murmured. 'It doesn't matter.'

'You, on the other hand,' he went on, 'are relatively inexperienced in these matters, and for your sake as well as mine I think it would be wise to...' He hesitated, as if groping for the right words. Then he shrugged. 'Well, to spell out a few guidelines.'

To her amazement, a dull red flush began to spread slowly over his face, and she realised that he was embarrassed by the speech he was making. And what in the world did he mean by 'guidelines'? It sounded as though they were going to enter into a business venture.

'I'm afraid I don't quite understand,' she said.

He sighed deeply, then gave her a rueful smile. 'That's probably because I'm explaining it very badly.' He took in a deep breath. 'The long and short of it is, Joanna, that I'm really basically monogamous at heart, and I'd like to keep our relationship exclusive. That is, see only each other, and that means no Martin Kingsley. Do you agree?'

Then it dawned on her. He was jealous! Stephen Ryan, jealous of Martin! 'Yes, Stephen, I do agree. It's what I want, too.'

Immediately, relief flooded into his face, and the tense muscles of his jaw visibly relaxed. He reached out to touch her face, his bright blue gaze filled with gratitude.

'I also want you to know,' he said softly, 'that I think you were probably right when you accused me of using my fears as a shield, a protection against making a commitment.'

'Stephen,' she said, 'I don't want to tie you down to something you're not ready for. I only want you to trust me.'

He lifted his shoulders in a gesture of resignation. 'I don't have any choice, actually. I have to trust you, your strength, your courage.' He gazed deeply into her eyes. 'I don't know where we're going, you and I, but I'm convinced it has to be together. I'm too much in love with you now to give you up.'

Joanna's heart filled so that she could hardly breathe. She smiled at him and raised his hand to press it against her cheek. 'I love you, too, Stephen,' she managed at last.

She couldn't speak. There was a choking sensation in her throat and her heart pounded wildly. She held her breath, watching as his head bent slowly towards her.

He kissed her again, deeply, urgently, his arms holding her close. As his tongue penetrated past her parted lips, probing, demanding, one hand slipped inside her blouse to touch her bare flesh. Her head fell back in a gesture of abandonment, and she yielded herself up to him completely, without reservation.

He lifted his head to gaze down at her. Then, in answer to the unasked question in his eyes, she rose to her feet and reached out a hand to him. Without a word, he rose up beside her, and she led him down the short hallway to her bedroom.

At the side of the bed, he took her in his arms and held her close for several moments. Then, smoothing back her hair, he cupped her chin in his hand and tilted her head back to look deeply into her eyes. Still holding her gaze in his, he reached behind her and slowly lowered the zip of her dress. When it had fallen to the floor at her feet, he bent his head to place his lips on her shoulder.

Joanna threw her arms around him, cradling him to her and pressing her cheek against the dark head as his mouth moved to the crook of her neck, then her other shoulder, and he began to tug gently but insistently at the straps of her lacy bra.

Joanna held her breath, then expelled a long sigh of pleasure as both his hands came to cover her bare breasts. She reached out to unbutton his shirt, then ran her hands inside it over his smooth, bare, muscled chest, where she could feel the heavy thud of his heartbeat.

In one deft movement he shrugged out of his shirt and pulled her up against him. His hands were everywhere now, in a frenzy of passion, on her breasts, her stomach, her back, clutching at her hips. As he pulled her against his hard body, his unmistakable thrusting need, a sudden awareness of her own power over him came to her then, almost awesome in its intensity. Her knees weakened and buckled under her, so that when he eased her down on the bed she slumped limply back on the pillow, her head whirling crazily, her pounding heart about to burst.

She raised her hips so that he could pull off the rest of her clothing, then closed her eyes and waited for him while he finished undressing, and in a moment his body came down to cover hers. She clung to him blindly as his hands and mouth continued to work their magic on her eager body, nuzzling and stroking her to a point of terrible, aching need, until finally she cried out to him and they were joined together at last.

## CHAPTER SEVEN

AFTERWARDS, Joanna slept deeply, dreamlessly, completely sated by Stephen's expert lovemaking, and it wasn't until the first early-morning light filtered in through the thin curtains at the window that her eyes fluttered open again and she gradually awakened. Stephen was still sleeping quietly beside her, lying on his stomach and breathing peacefully, the sheet tangled at his waist, his face turned towards her.

They were not quite touching, and as she watched the steady rise and fall of his shoulders she changed her position slightly, hardly moving at all, just to feel his skin against hers, the body so different from her own.

As she examined him in the brightness of the room, the wide shoulders, the broad planes of his hard-muscled back, she noticed that several scars marred the perfection of his smooth, tanned skin. There was one long welt just below his waist that could have been a knife wound, a small, round, puckered indentation on his left shoulder that could have been a bullet hole and other less formidable-looking marks that spoke of more minor injuries.

She stared down in horror, mesmerised by these potent reminders of his dangerous job. All the fears she had imagined she was beginning to conquer, for love of him, began to gnaw at her again. It was as though the night they'd just spent together, the tenderness and passion of their lovemaking, had altered her feelings for him in a fundamental way, committed her to him irrevocably. And made him a hundred times more precious to her.

Suddenly she realised that the rhythm of his breathing had changed, that one sleepy eye was open and fixed intently upon her. Their gaze met and held for several seconds, then he twisted around so that he was lying on his back, facing her. He reached out a hand to touch her hair, hanging loosely to her bare shoulders.

'I see you've noticed my battle scars,' he said quietly.

'Stephen . . .' she faltered. 'I had no idea. You never told me you'd been hurt.'

'It was a long time ago, when I was much younger and much less cautious.' He held out his arms to her and she nestled down beside him, her head in the crook of his neck. As he smoothed her hair back, he spoke in a soothing tone. 'You're not to worry about me, do you hear?' He gave her shoulders a reassuring squeeze, tilted her head up so that she was facing him and grinned down at her. 'I'm invincible.'

She smiled back at him, wanting to believe him, and determined once again to shake the heavy cloud of dread that filled her heart. 'All right, sir,' she replied playfully. 'If you say you're invincible, then I have no choice but to believe you.'

He smoothed her hair back from her forehead and kissed her lightly on the mouth. 'That's my girl.' Then the blue eyes glinted at her, and he pulled her closer. 'How are you, darling?' he asked in a low voice. 'Any regrets?'

'Not one,' she replied firmly. 'And I feel wonderful. But if we don't want to create a scandal, I think you'd better leave soon.' She glanced at the bedside clock. 'It's almost six o'clock.'

'Later,' he muttered, and lowered his head to nuzzle her neck. Then he breathed at her ear, 'If you're really worried about a scandal, I'll leave, but you'd better make up your mind quickly, before it's too late.'

'No,' she said, nestling against him. 'Don't go.'

His large hands began to travel over her body, and as his mouth moved to her breast she held his tousled dark head in her hands, pressing it to her. The feel of his crisp hair under her fingers, his unshaven face rasping sensuously on her bare skin, soon sent her soaring to the heights of desire once again.

Later, after showering and dressing, Joanna cooked breakfast for him. He sat at the table watching her, a light stubble on his unshaven jaw, his hair still damp, and wearing only his worn jeans, leaving his chest bare.

This was a Stephen entirely new to Joanna, relaxed, casual, unshaven, and as she cooked for him, served him, then sat across from him and watched him eat the bacon and eggs she had prepared, she wondered how she could ever have imagined she was happy with her old solitary life.

No wonder, she thought, women made such fools of themselves over men. She understood now how the presence of a man could become the focal point of a woman's existence. Stephen filled the small house with himself. It was a warmer, more alive place, just because he was in it.

She *had* conquered her fears, she vowed silently. Nothing would ever come between them now that she knew he loved her.

The next few weeks were the happiest Joanna had ever known. It was an especially beautiful summer, not oppressively hot or humid, and with clear blue skies well into June. Although she was always busy after Memorial Day, she still managed to spend every moment she could with Stephen.

True to his word, their relationship was totally exclusive. All his attention and passion were focused on her, and she basked in the delight he took in her, the intensity of his desire, the tenderness of his lovemaking. They had fallen naturally into the habit of discussing the future in terms of being together and, although no definite plans had been made, marriage seemed to be a foregone conclusion.

She was even getting used to the old scars that marred his perfection. She could touch them now without the old fears rising up immediately to haunt her. He'd said he was invincible and, although she knew he was only teasing, she half believed him, simply because she wanted to.

He was on night duty again this week, so she hadn't seen much of him, but he called her one Wednesday evening from his office to ask her to have dinner with him on Friday night.

'Maybe we can take in another movie in Panama City,' he added. 'That is, if you're up to it after the last one.'

'I'll tell you what,' she said. 'You've bought me dinner several times, and even cooked for me. Why don't I fix a meal for you instead?'

'You mean you can cook, too?'

She flushed warmly as she caught the meaning of that 'too', and said, 'Well, I'm no Elizabeth David, but I might surprise you.'

'OK, it sounds good. I'll see you on Friday, then, around seven o'clock.'

\*     \*     \*

By Friday, Joanna had worked herself into a near panic over her dinner menu. The truth was that she rarely cooked, had never really learned how, and after dithering around all morning going through the few cookbooks she owned and rejecting one complicated recipe after another, she finally slammed the last one shut and decided to go ahead and settle for a steak after all.

All men liked steak, she reasoned. She'd only be courting disaster if she chose something too ambitious for her meagre culinary expertise. She did, however, splurge and buy a new dress, another summer cotton, pink, with a wide square neckline and thin straps.

By seven o'clock that evening, everything was prepared, potatoes scrubbed and ready to go in the oven, the steaks marinating on the counter, fresh greens crisping and vodka martinis chilling in the refrigerator.

Joanna was all ready for him. As she gave her reflection one last glance in the bedroom mirror, she thought with satisfaction that not only did the new dress do marvellous things for her slim figure, but there was a new sparkle in her hazel eyes, a secret smile on her lips, a sort of glow in her creamy complexion.

It was amazing what love could do, she thought as she went into the kitchen to turn the meat in the marinade, and she hummed a little tune under her breath, fluffing up the pillows on the couch in the living-room on her way.

She sat down slowly and closed her eyes. Even now she could feel his strong arms around her, his mouth on hers. In comparison to that joy, everything else in life paled into insignificance.

Just then the sharp ping of the oven timer broke into her fantasy, and she jumped up and ran into the kitchen to put the potatoes in to bake.

It was already twenty minutes past seven, she noticed as she glanced at the oven clock. He had been due almost half an hour ago, and it wasn't like him to be late.

Just then the telephone rang, and when she answered it Stephen came on the line. He sounded harried.

'I'm sorry, Joanna,' he said. 'Something urgent has come up, and I'm not going to make it for dinner. I would have let you know sooner, but it's been a madhouse down here and this is the first chance I've had to call. I only have a minute.'

'Of course, Stephen,' she said quickly. 'I understand.'

'With a little luck, I might be able to make it later. Would that be OK?'

'Yes. I can save the steaks.' It was on the tip of her tongue to ask him if he would be in any danger, but instinct told her to leave it alone. Instead, she only said, 'Stephen, be careful.'

'I always am,' he replied breezily.

Well, she thought after they'd said goodbye and hung up, that's that. He's not coming. The carefully prepared dinner, the spotless house, the new dress, were all for nothing.

In the kitchen, she put plastic wrap over the dish of marinating meat, covered the potatoes with foil and put them both in the fridge. The greens would keep, but she poured the pitcher of martinis into a thermos.

With one last rueful glance at the pretty table she had set in the small dining alcove off the kitchen, the pewter candlesticks, her grandmother's silver and china gleaming, she settled down at her desk in the living-room to check over the second-quarter balance sheet she had brought from her office.

She worked steadily for some time, so engrossed in what she was doing that she hardly noticed when the sun went down, and it wasn't until her stomach gave a loud growl of protest that she suddenly realised she hadn't eaten a thing since lunch. She glanced at the digital clock on her desk and was astounded to see that it was almost nine-thirty. She'd been working for two hours. It was time to stop.

She stretched widely and shoved her chair back. Then, just as she rose to her feet, the doorbell chimed, echoing in the silence of the house. Her heart gave a great leap. He'd made it, after all! She ran to the door, pausing only to catch her breath and glance briefly into the hall mirror. Her hair was slightly disarranged and the dash of lipstick she'd put on earlier had long since been chewed off, but it didn't matter. He was here!

She smoothed down the skirt of the pink dress and opened the door. 'Come in, Stephen,' she said happily. 'I'm so glad you could make it.'

He gave her a weary, wintry smile. 'Don't you know you should never open your door at night like that without first finding out who's there?'

He stepped inside. Joanna closed the door and turned around to face him. It had only been a week since she'd last seen him, but tonight he seemed like a stranger to her. His usually impeccable dark suit was wrinkled, the top button of his shirt undone, his tie askew, and he needed a shave.

Then, as he came closer under the light, she could see that he looked exhausted. His lean face was haggard and drawn, and his broad shoulders slumped wearily forward. There were dark circles under his eyes, the normally bright blue dimmed with a dull greyish cast, and his dark hair fell untidily over his forehead.

'Come and sit down,' she said, leading the way into the living-room. 'I'll fix you a drink.'

He sank down on the couch, then leaned his head back and closed his eyes. She gazed down at him for a moment, suddenly filled with a powerful urge to reach down and smooth his hair back from his forehead, to comfort him in some way.

But she didn't want to disturb him. He seemed to be dead on his feet, half asleep already. Instead she went into the kitchen to get his drink. While she poured out his martini from the thermos she heard him call to her, and she turned around to see him standing at the kitchen door.

'I could use a wash,' he said.

'Bathroom's just down the hall,' she called back. 'You can't miss it.'

She carried the drinks tray back into the living-room, set it down on the coffee-table in front of the couch and sat down to wait for him. She had brought along the thermos. He looked as though one drink might not be quite enough.

When he returned a few minutes later, he looked more like himself. His hair was neatly combed again, his colour better, and a little of the old sparkle was back in his eyes. He sat down beside her and she handed him a glass. He raised it in the air.

'Here's to you, Joanna,' he said, and took a long swallow.

'Why to me?' she said. 'All I've done is sit at home, while you've been slaving away at—whatever.'

He gave her a long, silent look. 'That's all you need to do,' he said at last.

She put a hand on his arm. 'What happened?' she asked quietly. 'Can you tell me about it?'

'Are you sure you want to hear?'

Steeling herself, she nodded. 'I'm sure.' She wanted to hear about anything that concerned him.

'All right, then,' he went on, 'but first, you don't have an old crust of bread lying around, do you?'

She gazed at him in horror. 'You mean you haven't eaten?' He shook his head, and she started to laugh. 'Well, come to think of it, neither have I.' She stood up. 'Come into the kitchen and talk to me while I fix our dinner.'

With the potatoes baking in the microwave oven and the steaks sizzling under the broiler, Joanna tossed dressing into the salad and listened to Stephen telling her about the terrible events of the evening, about the teenage hoodlum who had been killed during an armed robbery and how powerfully it had affected him, even though he hadn't actually pulled the trigger himself.

He spoke steadily all through dinner in a low, controlled voice and, although Joanna was poignantly aware of the pain underlying his calm, dispassionate tone, it never faltered.

He didn't finish until she'd cleared the table and poured out their coffee. When the long, sad tale was over, Joanna leaned across the table towards him. She hadn't uttered a word while he was speaking, but now she knew she had to say something.

'Stephen, you didn't shoot that boy.'

He darted her a quick look. 'No,' he said curtly. 'Not this time. But it could have been me.'

'Yes,' she said softly. 'But someone has to do it, and better you than some insensitive clod who wouldn't care who got hurt. It's your job. You chose it.'

'Right,' he agreed. He put his elbows on the table and gazed intently at her. 'You know, Joanna, this will happen again. And next time I might be the one who has to pull that trigger, or someone will do it to me. You should be quite clear on that. If you're still squeamish about that aspect of my job, or the idea is repellent to you, then now's the time to face up to it.'

At the ominous tone, a cold chill passed through her, and she set her fork down carefully on her plate. 'Why are you telling me this? There's more to it, isn't there?'

The blue gaze narrowed. 'I haven't told you the worst of it.'

Joanna shivered. 'Then perhaps you'd better.'

'My partner was severely wounded tonight, shot through the chest right after he fired his own gun. The reason I was so late is because I stayed with him at the hospital, hoping for some word on his condition. His wife was there. They have three small children. He's not expected to live. How do you explain that to a wife and mother? What kind of life will she have without him?'

From the very beginning of his impassioned recitation, she was plunged back into the past, to that awful moment three years ago when she had received the news of Ross's death. Only this time it was a hundred times worse. Her mind began to form vivid pictures of Stephen shot, Stephen lying in the hospital near death. Gradually the scenario expanded to include herself, as his wife, with small children, facing a future without him.

By the time he was half-way through, a weird feeling of unreality had gripped her so that she only half listened to the end of his speech. She leaned back limply in her chair. All her bones seemed turned to jelly. She couldn't think, couldn't move, and was simply incapable of fighting down the growing panic that swept over her.

How would she feel when Stephen strapped that gun on again and went back out into those dangerous streets? What if it did happen to him? And even if it didn't, would she be able to tolerate the anxiety, the constant apprehension that it *might* happen?

As the waves of fear washed over her, she struggled for control. Her hands twisted in her lap as she tore her paper napkin into shreds. It would be all right, she kept assuring herself, over and over again, until finally she began to believe it.

Just then Stephen rose abruptly to his feet and stretched widely. He had taken off his suit jacket and loosened his tie when they sat down to dinner, and as Joanna looked up at him now, at the way the powerful muscles of his arms and shoulders strained against the thin material of his white shirt, her worry faded. Nothing could possibly happen to this strong man, so full of vitality.

He rubbed a hand over the back of his neck and gazed down at her. 'Well, Joanna, you've fed me and listened to me for hours, and now it's almost midnight. I'm dead beat, and you probably are, too. I think I'd better shove off now while I'm still able to drive. I'll call you.'

No, she thought, as he kissed her tenderly at the door, nothing bad would happen to him.

The minute he was gone, the house seemed so cold and empty, and as she walked slowly back to the kitchen to clear away their dinner things her doubts returned. What had possessed her to get involved with another policeman? When he was with her, he seemed so strong, so sure of himself that he seemed immortal.

Ross had been strong and confident, too, and ten years younger than Stephen when he was killed. That hadn't helped him.

Yet, even as she agonised over what might lay ahead, she knew in her heart that it was too late. She couldn't give Stephen up now even if she wanted to. She'd just have to forget her worries about his safety and concentrate on enjoying him. He was her fate, her destiny now.

The next day was Joanna's day off, but she went down to her hotel office just the same, on the principle that work was probably the best cure for the awful visions that had assailed her since Stephen had told her about the shooting last night—visions of Stephen hurt, shot, wounded and bleeding, perhaps at that very moment. Only work could distract her from the clammy hands, the pounding heart whenever those visions appeared.

She sat at her desk, staring down at a tall stack of folders that were filled with bits of unfinished business she had been postponing for weeks. She had just opened the top folder and started half-heartedly checking over the chef's list of the next week's dinner menus when Betty appeared at the door to her office.

'Shame on you,' the redhead clucked as she came inside. 'Working on your day off. Don't you ever take a holiday?'

'Oh, I had some things to catch up on. Maybe I'll take tomorrow off instead.' She leaned back in her chair and smiled. 'How about you? What are you doing here?'

'Not working, that's for sure. Have you got a minute?'

'Sure,' Joanna replied, waving her to the chair across the desk. 'Sit down.'

As Betty came forward, she made a great show of waving one hand in the air. The sun pouring in through the window glinted on one finger, setting off a brilliant spark from a very large square-cut diamond ring.

'Betty!' Joanna cried. 'Don't tell me! Edward?'

'Can you believe it? After all these years of swearing he'd never marry again, he suddenly decides it's not such a bad idea after all to spend his declining years with his faithful—um—secretary.'

'That's wonderful, Betty. When is it to be?'

'Some time early next month. You know how men are. Now that he's finally made up his mind, he's convinced himself it's all his idea and is in a mad rush to get it done as soon as possible.'

'What do you suppose brought it about?' Joanna asked, then raised a hand in the air. 'No, don't tell me. It was the robbery, getting hurt, the time he spent in the hospital.'

'You've got it,' Betty said with a smirk. 'Made him realise none of us is going to live forever. Not even Edward Morgan.'

At this reminder of her own worry over Stephen's safety, Joanna shivered a little and closed her eyes. When she opened them again, Betty was gazing at her with a penetrating, narrow-eyed stare.

'What's wrong with you, Joanna?' she asked gruffly.

'Nothing's wrong. Why do you ask?'

'You look terrible. Positively ill, in fact.'

Joanna laughed. 'Well, thanks a lot.'

'Sorry. You know me. I call 'em the way I see 'em. Never did have any tact.' She leaned forward, peering intently into Joanna's face. 'Maybe you have a touch of our famous summer flu.'

'No,' Joanna replied with a shake of her head. 'I'm never sick.'

Betty snorted and crossed her legs with a rustle of stiff silk skirt. 'Well, those circles under your eyes don't exactly make you look like the picture of health to me. Come on, now, Joanna,' she went on in a softer tone. 'We've been friends for too long to play games with each other now. Give.'

Joanna opened her mouth, then closed it again. She wanted to talk about it, she trusted Betty, but something held her back.

Betty cocked her head to one side. 'Is it Stephen?'

Suddenly, Joanna's throat closed up, and the hot tears stung behind her eyelids. She reached for a tissue from the box on her desk and blew her nose. Then she nodded and forced out a weak smile.

'See what you've done?' she said shakily when she could find her voice again. 'That's what sympathy always does to me.'

'Do you want to talk about it?'

Joanna shook her head. 'Not really. There's nothing to talk about, actually. I just didn't sleep very well last night.'

'I was afraid of this,' Betty said quietly.

Joanna widened her eyes. 'Afraid of what?'

'That Stephen's job would rake up all the bad memories.'

Joanna rose from her chair and walked over to gaze outside. Several guests of the hotel were down on the beach, and the happy laughter of children at play drifted in through the open window. The tide was rolling in gently, and the hot sun beat down on the glaring white sand. Far off on the southern horizon, small greyish-white clouds were gathering.

She slowly turned around. 'You've known Stephen a long time, Betty,' she said carefully.

'Since he was born,' was the prompt reply.

Joanna came around the desk to stand before her. 'Then you must know why he's never married, or made a permanent commitment.'

'Well, I know what he's always *said*. But I also think he's finally met the one woman who could change his mind.' She gave Joanna a closer look. 'What is it? Is he still worried you'll try to talk him into giving up his work?'

Joanna sat back on the edge of the desk. 'Well, what would be so terrible about that? He could go back to the practice of law,' she said eagerly. 'It would be so simple. He's already passed the Bar. He has all his credentials, several years' experience——'

'And hated every minute of it,' Betty broke in drily. 'He always wanted to be a policeman at heart. If you know him at all **by** now, you must be aware that he's got a mighty firm character. Once he makes his mind up to a thing, that's it. He was that way as a boy, and still is, as far as I can see.'

'But surely it couldn't hurt to ask him,' Joanna said.

Betty eyed her carefully. 'He might do it for you—he's obviously mad about you—but you'd be taking a risk.'

'How do you mean?'

Betty rose to her feet with a sigh. 'Surely you must realise that a man like Stephen hasn't wanted for feminine companionship all these years, and I'm not telling tales out of school about that. It's common knowledge among the local belles that he was strictly off limits as far as a serious relationship went. Now, ask yourself—why is it that a man like that, very attractive to women and certainly not a monk, has never even come close to marriage?'

Joanna's heart sank. 'His work,' she said dully.

Betty nodded. 'Right. He's a man who doesn't make commitments easily, but when he does, they're engraved in stone. I just can't see him giving up the job that means so much to him.' She shrugged her heavy shoulders. 'But don't take my word for it. People do change—look at Edward—and if he'd do it for anybody, he'd do it for you.'

Joanna thought this over for a moment, then said, 'Well, tell me this. Do you think it would do any harm to feel him out on the subject?'

Betty braced her hands on the arms of the chair and heaved herself to her feet. 'Honey, I just don't know. He's such a private person. You know him in a way I never could.' She gave Joanna's arm a reassuring squeeze. 'You love him, don't you?'

Joanna smiled weakly. 'I'm afraid so.'

'Then you want what's best for him. Why not just let your instinct be your guide?' She shrugged and gave Joanna a sly grin. 'I can't see that it would hurt to ask, though.'

'Thanks, Betty. I'll think about it.' They walked together slowly towards the door. 'And congratulations again. I'm so happy for you both.'

When Betty had gone, Joanna returned to the menus on her desk, but it didn't take long to convince her that the effort was hopeless, and after a few minutes she pushed them away with a sigh. She leaned her head back and closed her eyes.

Betty had told her to trust her instincts, but how could she be sure which were the right ones? She loved him, she *did* want what was best for him, but she also wanted him alive and in one piece.

## CHAPTER EIGHT

THE next morning Joanna was awakened out of a sound sleep by the shrill ringing of the telephone beside her bed. She opened one eye and glanced at the clock. It was only seven-thirty. With a groan, she raised up on one elbow and reached for the telephone.

'Hello,' she muttered groggily.

'Joanna, it's Stephen. Sorry to call you so early, but my partner died during the night, and I need to stop by to pay my respects to his widow. It's a very unpleasant chore, but it's got to be done.' He hesitated briefly, then said, 'Would you come with me?'

She recoiled instinctively from the thought of what it might do to her to have to face another grieving police widow, but she quickly fought it down. 'Of course, Stephen. I'll be glad to. When do you want to go?'

'Will an hour give you enough time?'

'Yes. I'll be ready.'

When they hung up, she lay back on the pillows, still fighting the clamouring panic his request had set raging through her. She was ashamed of her cowardice, but unable to help herself. She knew she should be pleased that he wanted her to go with him to visit his partner's widow. He even seemed to need her help with his awful duty. She simply had to get on top of this sudden awful fear.

It was a grim-faced Stephen who appeared on her doorstep at eight-thirty sharp, and the drive into

Pensacola was largely a silent one. He sat beside her, his jaw set, his blue eyes half shut, intent on the road ahead.

The cottage was in a quiet district of small timber houses. In the front yard on the small patch of lawn there was a child's tricycle, and a baby carriage sat on the covered front porch. Joanna felt a sharp pang of terrible pity at this evidence of children—and very young children, from the looks of it.

Stephen switched off the engine, pulled on the hand-brake and turned to her. 'I've had to do this a few times in the past,' he said bleakly, 'and always dreaded it.' He leaned over to brush a light kiss on her mouth. 'I can't tell you how much it means to me to have you with me.'

She forced out a weak smile and squeezed his hand tightly. They got out of the car and walked slowly up the path. When they reached the front door, Stephen took a deep breath and rang the bell. From inside there came the sound of a baby crying, and Joanna had to fight down a fresh attack of nerves.

Finally the door was opened by a slim young girl with flaming red hair. When she saw Stephen, she pushed open the screen. It was obvious she'd been crying. Her small pointed face was ashen, and she seemed to be holding herself together with an effort.

'Hello, Stephen,' she said shakily, holding the door open for them. 'Please come in.'

As they stepped into the small, cluttered living-room, a cold shiver went up Joanna's spine, and her knees threatened to buckle under her. When Ross was killed, his partner had come to her on just such a mission, and the painful memory still had the power to unnerve her.

Stephen took the girl's hands in his. 'I'm so sorry, Mary,' he said softly. 'Bert and I had been together for a long time. I'll miss him. We all will.'

The girl made a brave attempt at a smile. 'Thanks, Stephen. It was good of you to come.'

He turned to Joanna. 'Mary, this is my fiancée, Joanna Barnes. Joanna, Mary Sinclair.'

The two women looked at each other, and in the haunted eyes of the young widow Joanna saw her own reflection. The cold chill seemed to have paralysed her into a block of solid granite. She didn't think she would be able to speak a word or move a muscle to save her life. She could only stand there staring blindly down at Mary Sinclair as wave after wave of unreasoning terror began to sweep over her.

This young woman couldn't be any older than she had been herself when Ross was killed. Mary Sinclair was a carbon copy of the girl she had been—lost, insecure, terrified by the thought of life alone, but trying desperately to put on a brave front, just as she had, and she didn't think she could bear it.

Then she realised that both Mary and Stephen were staring at her. She had to say something. Fighting back the panic, she finally found her voice.

'I'm so sorry, Mrs Sinclair,' she said. 'I know how terrible this is for you.'

The girl nodded and the bright tears glistened in her eyes. 'Thank you,' she murmured.

'Mary, if there's anything I can do,' Stephen said, 'anything at all, please call on me.'

Just then the baby they'd heard when they had first arrived started to cry again, and Mary raised her head abruptly, listening. 'Excuse me a minute,' she said. 'I have to see to Timmy.'

When she was gone, Joanna lost all pretence of holding herself together for the girl's sake. Her mind suddenly went blank, and she felt herself swaying on her feet. A bitter nausea rose up into her throat, and she reached out blindly for support as the blackness started to close in on her.

Then she felt Stephen's arm come around her, and heard him speaking low into her ear. 'Joanna, what is it?'

The sound of his voice penetrated the fog in her head, and his strong arm gave her the support she needed. She leaned against him and blinked up at him. His face swam before her, then slowly came into focus, full of concern. She had to do something, say something, before he could guess what was happening to her.

Just then Mary Sinclair came back into the room carrying the sobbing child, patting him on the back and making soothing noises. Joanna moved away from the shelter of Stephen's arm, and immediately her head began to whirl again.

'I—I'm sorry,' she stammered. 'I think I'd better wait outside.'

She turned and walked as slowly and steadily as she could towards the door, which seemed like a million miles away, certain she would collapse at each faltering step. When she finally made it outside, she closed the door quietly behind her and drew in several lungfuls of air, until she finally felt able to go on.

She stumbled blindly down the path to the car, and when she was inside she rolled down the window, then lowered her head between her legs to get the blood flowing back into it. After a few minutes, she began to feel a little better. The nausea was ebbing away and her head was clearing, but the awful anxiety was stubbornly hanging on. She rested her pounding head back on the seat and put a hand over her heart in a vain attempt to still heavy thudding.

She felt so ashamed! How could she have given in to the old weakness that way? Would she never be free of it? She'd been so sure it was over. Now she felt like running away and hiding, or smashing something. Her heart ached for poor Mary Sinclair, and her one feeble hope was that she hadn't made things worse for her. She'd have to come back alone another day and try to make it up to her.

Then she heard Stephen's slow footsteps coming down the path, heard him open his door and settle himself behind the steering wheel. She opened her eyes to see that he was staring intently at her, a puzzled frown on his face.

'What happened in there, Joanna?' he said at last. 'You were white as a sheet. I thought you were going to pass out any minute. You still look terrible.'

She forced out a brittle laugh. 'Well, thank you. That's very flattering.'

'Well, what is it?' he persisted. He reached out a hand towards her, then let it drop. 'Are you ill?'

He was obviously not going to let it go. She had to tell him something. 'Maybe I am catching something. Betty said just the other day there's a lot of summer flu going around.'

'Shouldn't you be in bed, then?'

'Oh, Stephen, honestly, it's nothing at all.'

He continued to stare at her for a second or two, then nodded, as though satisfied with her explanation. 'Stubborn little thing, aren't you?' He grinned and shook his head slowly from side to side. 'What am I going to do with you, Joanna?'

His tone was playful, but she couldn't miss the seriousness underlying it, and she was glad when he started the car and headed along the beach road back towards Miramar.

As they drove along, he spoke of Mary Sinclair's loss, and as he told her about the fund the police department was setting up to help her over the worst of her difficulties her spirits gradually revived.

'You really care, don't you, Stephen?' she said when he was through.

He darted her a startled glance. 'Of course I care. Who wouldn't?'

Joanna wondered how she ever could have thought he was a cold man. The iron reserve was only a protective mask, probably adopted out of necessity in order to cope with the ugly demands of his work. Beneath it was a sensitive, caring man, a good man.

Too good, she thought, to spend every working hour on the cutting edge of danger. Each time he went out on a job could be the last, and it wasn't right, wasn't fair that he should have to be the one to do it.

Today's encounter with Mary Sinclair had convinced her, too, how vulnerable she was to the dangers he faced. Not only was Stephen too valuable a human being to be thrown away, but she shouldn't have to live in constant dread of losing him. It made no sense at all.

Gradually her resolve strengthened, and by the time they arrived at the hotel and were walking up the steps to her cottage she had made up her mind. Turning to him, she gave him a bright smile and put a hand on his arm.

'Stephen, I've been thinking. How would you like to take a trip up to Boston with me to meet my parents?'

He raised his eyebrows. 'Well, sure,' he said slowly. 'I'd like that.' Then he frowned. 'What brought that on all of a sudden?'

'Well, I'm proud of you and want to show you off. And while we're there, you could talk to my father about his law practice. You know, I told you he needed help.'

The frown deepened. 'Why would I want to do that, Joanna?'

'Well, what would be so wrong with giving the law another chance? If Boston doesn't appeal to you, you wouldn't even have to leave Miramar. Martin is so busy. I'll bet he'd be glad to take you on as a partner. You haven't been away for that long, and——'

'Joanna!' His voice broke into her nervous, rambling speech like a gunshot. 'Look at me.'

She had been gazing at a point just in the centre of his forehead. Now, at his harsh tone, she dropped her eyes to meet his. When she saw the stern, forbidding look on his face, her heart gave a sickening lurch.

'Joanna,' he said in a gentler tone. 'We've discussed this before. You know how much you mean to me. I love you. I want to marry you. But I've got to be free to do the work I've committed myself to. I thought you understood that.'

'I do understand it, Stephen. It's just that——' She broke off helplessly.

'Do you love me, Joanna?' he asked softly.

'Of course I do. You know that.'

'Then it will work itself out. Trust me. Trust yourself, your own instincts.'

She knew he was right, knew too that if she didn't drop the subject she'd say too much, go too far. But the haunting image of Mary Sinclair still obsessed her, and she couldn't stop herself.

'It's because I love you that I'm asking you at least to consider it,' she went on excitedly. 'And I am trusting my instincts. Don't you see? What they tell me is that I don't want to lose you the way I lost Ross, the way Mary lost her husband, not if there's a chance you might be just as happy in a safer job.' Her voice broke, and she reached out blindly for him.

He pulled back from her and gave her a narrow look. 'Tell me, Joanna,' he said in a flat, cold tone, 'doesn't it strike you as odd that your sudden "illness" came right on the heels of my partner's death? And that today, out of the blue, you're trying to push me back into the law?'

She knew then that she'd gone too far, and she forced out a shaky smile. 'Well, I guess it's possible that there might be a connection, but I don't think it's very important. You're all right, after all. And I wasn't pushing you, I just thought you might consider changing jobs, but I can see you're still opposed to it. Let's just forget it.'

'And what about next time?'

'Next time?'

'You do realise that what happened last night could happen again, don't you? And that next time it could be me that gets shot—and you'd be the one sitting in the hospital waiting to hear if I'm alive or dead?'

'Why, yes. We talked about that before, and I told you . . .'

'I know what you told me,' he said in a harsh voice. 'But I think now you were lying to me—or to yourself.'

'Stephen, don't. You're making too much of this.' A slow anger began to rise up in her at his tone. She pulled back from him and gave him a challenging look. 'Have you ever considered the possibility that you're the one who's being a little unreasonable here? Even,' she added, 'a bit selfish?'

'There's always that possibility,' he said evenly. 'But it doesn't change anything.'

'Why do I have to do all the adapting?' she said, her voice rising with her temper. 'Why is it out of the question for you to even consider going back to the law? Why can't you think about *my* feelings for a change?'

'Because you've spent the last few weeks assuring me that you were overcoming those feelings, those fears,' he ground out.

His face was like thunder, and for one second she was certain he was going to hit her. But by now she didn't even care. Her great love affair lay in ruins around her, and nothing else seemed to matter.

They stood there glaring at each other, neither giving an inch, until finally his shoulders slumped and he gave her a look of utter defeat.

'It won't work, will it?' he asked bleakly. 'I should have known it wouldn't work. There's too much history, isn't there? I think we'd better just forget the whole thing. You can stay in your safe little world, but it'll have to be without me.'

He raised a hand, as though to reach out for her, but in the next moment he dropped it helplessly at his side. He gave her one last, long look, then turned abruptly and strode off down the path.

She watched his retreating figure until he reached his car, aching to call him back, but knowing it would be useless. She heard the engine fire, and stood there helplessly, her hand at her throat, watching him drive off.

In the next few agonising weeks, Joanna went over and over that parting scene in her mind. In late June the Gulf Coast suffered an unusual spell of cloudy weather, which only made the long, dreary days without Stephen seem even worse. There were even times when she looked back at her old worries over his safety with nostalgia. Anything would be better than the awful knowledge that she would never see him again, never lie in his arms, never feel his warm breath on her mouth.

He didn't call. Although she hadn't really expected him to, she still nursed a little ray of hope that he might change his mind, still felt a quickening of her heartbeat whenever the telephone rang, hoping beyond reason for the sound of his deep, quiet voice.

There were times when she had to get up from her desk, at home or in her office, and pace around the room to keep from picking up the telephone and calling him. The only thing that really stopped her was that she knew quite well it was too late. He was a man of firm decision and iron will. When he'd said it was over between them, that was it.

Her one consolation during those awful weeks was that, if it hurt this badly now, how much worse it would have been to have lost him if they had married. She tried to convince herself that she was really no worse off now than she was before Stephen Ryan came into her life. She still had her work, her friends, her family.

All that was cold comfort to her, however, when she was lying in bed alone at night with the feel of his mouth still on her lips and his hands on her body.

She would get over it in time, she told herself as she plodded through the long hours without him. She'd only known him a few months, not long enough for him to have captured a permanent place in her heart.

Betty and Edward were to be married on a Sunday afternoon in early July, with only Joanna, Karen and Martin in attendance. A grand reception would follow the ceremony afterwards in Edward's suite in the hotel. Stephen would probably be there, and Joanna's first instinctive reaction, of course, was to beg off going when Betty told her about it the Thursday afternoon beforehand.

But Betty would have none of that. 'Now, listen, Joanna,' she said severely, 'you've got to come. We've all been very patient with you and left you alone, but it's been almost a month now, and you have to make a little effort yourself. You can't just resign from the human race over one unhappy love affair. We've all had them. I've had one or two myself, but stayed in there pitching, and look at how well it's turned out for me. Besides, Stephen may not even come.'

In spite of herself, Joanna had to laugh. She also felt a little guilty. Betty was right. Even though a celebration was the farthest thing from her mind, she knew she should at least put in an appearance, for her friends' sake, if nothing else.

'I'm sorry, Betty,' she said at last. 'Of course I'll come.'

'Good.' The redhead hesitated for a moment, then cautiously said, 'I know Martin will be very glad to hear that.'

Joanna stared. 'Martin! What does he have to do with it?'

'Martin has always been very fond of you.'

Joanna laughed aloud. 'Martin Kingsley is fond of anything in skirts. Besides, I thought he and Karen Morgan had a thing going.'

Betty reddened deeply and turned away. 'Not any more,' she mumbled. 'Not since——' She broke off and gave Joanna a look of sheer misery.

Although she knew what was coming, Joanna had to find out for sure. 'Not since what, Betty? Come on. You've got to finish it now.'

Betty shifted her position uncomfortably. 'Well, all right. She's always had her cap set for Stephen, ever since she was a young girl.' She laughed shortly. 'For all the good it did her. Honestly, Joanna, it doesn't mean a thing. He was probably the one man on the whole northern Gulf Coast from Pensacola to Panama City who wasn't taken in by her, and she sees him as a sort of trophy.'

Joanna could hardly believe the feeling of desolation that seized her at the very thought of Karen and Stephen together. Well, she thought, I don't have much left, but I can at least hang on to a little pride.

She lifted her chin. 'It's not my business any more. Stephen is a free agent. He doesn't want me anyway. Maybe Karen will have better luck with that stiff-necked, stubborn——'

'Hey,' Betty put in with a laugh, 'I know how you feel. Men! They're all alike. But you will still come to the reception?'

'Of course.'

'And, Joanna, don't reject Martin too hastily. He has a lot to offer a woman. He's attractive, he has money, and I think he's ready to settle down. He also has a nice safe job, which I know is important to you.'

Joanna gave her a swift, suspicious glance. 'I was perfectly willing to put up with Stephen's job, Betty,' she said stiffly. 'You know it and so does he. He's the one who sent me away, after all.'

Betty rolled her eyes heavenward. 'Oh, Joanna, I'm sorry. I didn't mean it like that. I'd like to smack Stephen Ryan, as a matter of fact, for not giving you more of a chance to get over your fears gradually. He expects too much.'

'Oh, don't blame him,' Joanna said wearily. 'I understand what was in his mind. If a policeman has to worry about his wife's nerves, he'd be even more vulnerable to danger on the job than he already is.'

'Well, I'm sorry it didn't work out for you, but I know it doesn't help much.' As she turned to go down the hall to her office, she called over her shoulder, 'Think over what I said about Martin. I don't expect you to fall in love with him overnight, but he's good-looking and amusing, and it'll do you good to realise there *are* other men in the world.'

Joanna spent most of Friday and Saturday dreaming up excuses to get out of going to the reception, but nothing really convincing came to her, no matter what wild tales she concocted. Short of a raging fever or a broken leg, Betty would realise she was lying anyway.

She'd just have to go. It might even give her a lift to get out of the cold, lonely cottage. Lately it had seemed as though the walls were closing in on her.

The Sunday of the wedding was a lovely day, warm and sunny, and, surveying her depressing wardrobe, Joanna decided to wear the apricot dress she'd bought for Stephen. Not only was it the closest thing to a party dress she owned, but she knew it looked good on her, and she needed all the confidence she could muster if she was going to have to face him again.

The wedding itself was short, held at the small chapel in Miramar, and when it was over they all drove together in Martin's car back to the hotel for the reception.

Betty put everybody to work immediately. Even though the food was catered from the dining-room and Mrs Murphy had provided a bartender and one of the regular uniformed maids to help serve, there was still plenty to do before the other guests arrived, and Joanna was glad to be busy.

Soon the suite began to fill with people—the entire hotel staff, old friends of Edward's and Betty's from Miramar and the surrounding towns—until by four o'clock there was quite a crowd. Betty had arranged things so that there was conversation in the living-room, food laid out on the dining-room table, a bar in the kitchen, and dancing out on the wide balcony. It was very noisy, with music playing in the background and, as the drinks flowed freely, louder and louder chatter and laughter.

To cope with her nerves, Joanna had two rather stiff drinks right after the ceremony, and as they took effect she actually started to enjoy herself. She was in the dining-room talking to Mario and Andy when Martin strolled in from the kitchen, carrying a drink.

He marched directly over to her, grasped her hand in both of his and flashed her a wide grin. 'Joanna,' he said, slurring the word slightly, 'I've been meaning to tell you all afternoon how gorgeous you look in that sexy dress.'

He took her other hand and held her away from him, his arms wide, his eyes raking her up and down as though she were an actress auditioning for a part.

Joanna didn't know quite how to take this blatant appraisal, and she shifted uncomfortably under his minute scrutiny.

'I can't believe it,' he said with a solemn shake of his head. 'You look marvellous.' He was still holding her hands. 'You know, you ought to wear that kind of dress more often. You look good enough to eat.'

Joanna laughed nervously. 'Oh, come on, Martin. You're embarrassing me.'

'Well, I don't want to do that,' he said, tucking her arm under his and leading her towards the bar in the kitchen. 'It's just that I only see you on the job, and you always look so—so—*efficient*,' he finally managed. He drew her closer up against his side and breathed whisky fumes at her.

They were at the bar now, and he handed her a drink. 'I hear you and Stephen have broken your engagement,' he said in a low, confidential tone.

'Well, it was hardly an engagement,' she said and took a sip of her drink. 'But whatever it was, yes, it's over.'

He leaned his narrow hips back against the kitchen counter and gazed thoughtfully at her, his brow furrowed in concentration. 'You know how much I've always admired you, Joanna.'

Suddenly she recalled vividly the day last spring when they'd eaten lunch together in the coffee-shop, and the blonde in the bikini had walked by. He had wolfed down his lunch then, hardly able to get down to the beach fast enough.

'Martin,' she said with a laugh, 'does the woman exist you don't admire?'

Yes, she thought, watching him, Betty was right. She'd forgotten what a good-looking man he was. Now, for some reason, he was going out of his way to ingratiate himself with her, and she had to wonder why. Had Karen dumped him for Stephen and was now giving him to her as a sort of consolation prize?

She took another sip of her drink, a longer one this time, and the liquor went directly to her head. Martin's face became a little blurry. What difference did it make why he was suddenly turning serious on her? She was enjoying his attentions. And why not?

He was looking at her empty glass. 'How about a refill?'

She hesitated. She already felt a little wobbly. Then she thought again, why not? She was having a good time, the first in weeks. She handed him her glass. 'Sure,' she said.

He had just left her to cross over to the bar when she looked up to see Karen coming into the kitchen. As soon as the blonde girl caught sight of her standing there alone, she bounced immediately over to her side.

'Joanna,' she called as she came, 'is Martin trying to seduce you?'

Joanna laughed. 'Probably. He's an expert——'

She broke off when she saw Karen's gaze shift past her towards the living-room entrance, but before she could turn around to see what she found so fascinating Karen flashed her a triumphant smile.

'Well,' she said smugly, 'look who's here.'

Even before Joanna saw him, she knew it was Stephen, and she steeled herself. Sobering instantly, she looked around wildly for a place to hide, but when nothing presented itself she decided she'd just have to face it. It was bound to happen sooner or later.

Then, when his dark head appeared in the doorway, she began to tremble uncontrollably. It was as though a deep chasm had opened at her feet and she was about to fall in.

While Karen dashed immediately to his side, Joanna turned her head away quickly so he wouldn't see her staring at him. In the next moment she groaned inwardly as Martin came marching towards her with her drink. He stood directly in her line of vision, blocking her view of Stephen—and, thank heaven, his of her.

She took the glass from Martin and gulped half of it down. The drink helped, and when he moved to stand beside her all she could see was the back of Stephen's head as he disappeared back into the living-room, with Karen hanging on his arm and gazing up adoringly into his face.

In the meantime, Martin's arm had snaked around behind her, and as his grasp tightened on her waist she leaned against him, as though he might offer her some protection against the turmoil of emotion set up in her by the sight of Stephen.

'Would you like to dance?' he whispered in her ear.

She turned to him. His face was very close to hers, alarming her a little, but she did want to get out of that kitchen before Stephen came back. 'Yes,' she said, and with his arm firmly gripping her around her shoulders they made their way out on to the balcony.

It was a little chilly outside, and before long the cool evening air cleared Joanna's head. Gradually, she became aware of how tightly Martin was holding her and how she was clinging to him, with both arms around his neck.

Now, as she felt his hand begin to move slowly up and down her back, she wasn't so sure she needed that kind of support. She tried to pull away from him, but he only held her tighter, pressing hard against her. This won't do at all, she thought. She'd been grateful enough for Martin's solid presence a few minutes ago, at that first sight of Stephen, but now she began to worry that, in Martin's mind, she had been promising more than she had any intention of delivering.

She pulled her head back and looked up at him warily. His eyes were half closed and he had that dreamy, self-satisfied look on his face that certain men got when they were closing in for the kill. As she stared at him, she wondered how she could ever have thought him handsome.

He was a weak and shallow man, she realised. He always had been. He hadn't an ounce of character in his face, no matter how good a lawyer he might be. Somehow she had to get rid of him. It was getting late. If she could distract him somehow, she'd try to slip away from the party and go back to the safety and seclusion of her own cottage.

'Martin,' she said in a low, intimate tone, 'you know what I'd like?'

His eyes fluttered open and he pressed his cheek against hers. 'Mmm?' he murmured in her ear. 'What would you like? I'll bet it's the same thing I'd like.'

'I'd like another drink,' she said sweetly. 'Would you be a dear and get me one?'

He drew back and gazed down at her with a fatuous, confident smirk. 'Dutch courage?' he asked with the lift of one eyebrow.

She only smiled demurely and lowered her eyes. He chuckled deep in his throat. 'Don't go away,' he said, releasing her at last. 'I'll be right back.'

The minute he disappeared into the kitchen, Joanna made a dash for the door into the living-room. It was terribly smoky and very noisy inside, and jammed with people, all of whom seemed to be talking and laughing at once. She pushed her way through the crowd to the front door, where she was stopped cold by a large cluster of newcomers just entering.

She stood there literally wringing her hands with frustration and making a hopeless effort to squeeze her way through them to the door, when she suddenly heard a familiar voice behind her. She turned slowly around.

'Hello, Joanna,' Stephen said.

'Hello, Stephen.' She looked past him, but there was no sign of either Karen or Martin. 'How have you been?'

'Quite well, and you?'

'Oh, fine.' There was a short awkward silence. 'Well, I was just leaving...' she began.

'So soon?' He quirked a dark eyebrow at her. 'Won't Martin be disappointed?'

She bridled at that. 'Well, if it comes to that, what will Karen think when she sees you talking to me? Are you allowed to do that?'

His expression darkened, and he glowered down at her. Then he sighed. 'What's the point in wrangling like this?' he said bleakly. 'I'd hoped we could be friends, even though...' His voice trailed off, and he made an impotent gesture with one hand in the air.

'Yes, well, if I ever need a policeman, I'll be sure to call on you. Now, I really must go.'

The group at the door had finally dispersed. She gave him a thin smile, turned from him and walked outside.

If she'd needed any proof that it was really over, she thought on her way up the path to her cottage, she'd had it today. Not only did he seem to be properly hooked by the luscious Karen, but he'd made it quite clear that he was sticking to his guns about their ruined love affair. Friends, indeed! How could they ever be friends after what they'd been to each other?

Inside her own living-room, she kicked off her high heels and padded down to the bedroom to take off her dress, the dress she'd bought for Stephen. It seemed like a hundred years ago. Slipping on a robe, she padded down the hall back to the living-room, went over to her desk and took out the album of wedding photographs for the last time. After turning the pages listlessly for a few minutes, she closed it up and put it back in the drawer.

The past was gone, never to be recaptured; the present was terrible; and, as for the future, it didn't bear thinking about. She was all alone, and it looked as though she'd have to make up her mind to stay that way—forever. *That* seemed to be her true destiny, like it or not.

## CHAPTER NINE

EARLY one evening a week after Betty's marriage to Edward Morgan, Joanna was standing at the living-room window of her cottage, looking out at the pouring rain. The beach looked sodden, the sea a dull slate-grey, and the tall palms drooped sadly under the weight of water on their branches.

She felt restless and vaguely depressed. Nothing on the television appealed to her, she'd read every magazine in the place several times over, Betty and Edward were not in the mood for company, and she even considered calling Martin to see if he wanted to go to a movie. Anything, just so she wouldn't have to be alone with her thoughts.

What she needed was to get away. Everything here reminded her of Stephen. She hadn't had a good visit with her parents for a long time. They'd be glad to see her. On a sudden impulse she went over to the telephone on her desk and dialled their number in Boston.

She listened impatiently, tapping her foot, at the ringing in her ear. Five times, eight, then ten. Finally, there was a click, and her father answered in his usual cautious telephone voice.

'Hello?' he asked suspiciously.

There was so much noise in the background that she could hardly hear him. It sounded as though they were having a party, with music and laughter. 'Hello, Dad,' she said. 'It's Joanna.'

'Oh, hello, honey. How are you?'

'I'm OK. Listen, Dad, what's all that racket?'

'We just have a few friends in.' There was a long pause. Then he said, 'Why are you calling, Joanna? Is something wrong?'

'No, Dad. Everything's fine. I just wanted to hear the sound of your voice.' A lump started to form in her throat, and the tears smarted behind her eyes. 'I was just thinking I might come up there soon for a short visit.'

'Good, honey. We'd like that.'

The background noise escalated, and she heard someone call his name. 'Listen, Dad, I'd better hang up. I'll let you know later if I'll be able to get away.'

'Don't you want to say hello to your mother?'

'No. Just tell her I called and give her a big hug for me. One for you, too.'

They hung up then, and Joanna sniffed audibly in the empty room. Even her parents didn't care about her.

She reached in her jacket pocket for a tissue, but before the first gush of tears could well forth the telephone on the desk shrilled loudly. Glad of an interruption to her gloomy thoughts, she quickly snatched up the receiver.

'Hello,' she said eagerly.

'Mrs Barnes? Joanna Barnes?' came a woman's voice.

'Yes, speaking.'

'This is Laura Blake. You probably don't remember me. We met once briefly after the robbery at your hotel. I worked with Stephen Ryan on the case.'

A picture flashed into Joanna's mind of the tall blonde policewoman who had come with Stephen to question her that day. She also recalled her impression that Laura Blake had exhibited more than professional interest in him.

'Yes, of course,' she said. 'I do remember you.'

'I don't want to alarm you,' she went on, 'but Stephen has been hurt. Shot during a hold-up, as a matter of fact.'

'Shot?' Joanna murmured weakly. Her knees buckled under her, and a wave of dizziness passed over her. All the blood seemed to be draining out of her head, and she sank down on a nearby chair.

'There was a bank robbery in Pensacola this afternoon,' came the clipped, businesslike voice. 'Stephen and I were on the case together and he got in the line of fire.'

'How—how badly is he hurt?' Joanna finally managed to choke out.

'There's no way of knowing yet. He was shot twice, once in the chest and once in the leg. I'm at the hospital now. They just took him into surgery.'

Joanna's head began to clear, and it was then that she recognised the note of hostility in Laura's tone. It had been there from her first word. She also wondered why she was calling her. Then hope rose within her. Had Stephen asked for her? But there was no time for questions now. She had to go to him.

'Which hospital?'' she asked.

'Pensacola General.'

'I'll be right there,' Joanna said in a tight voice.

'There's really no hurry. The doctors say that he'll be unconscious for quite a while after the surgery.' She hesitated briefly, then added, 'I just thought you should know.'

That didn't sound much as though Stephen had asked for her. 'Thank you for calling, Laura,' she said.

After they'd hung up, Joanna sat for several moments trying to think. If only she could stop *shaking* so!

Stephen! she thought. Lying in a hospital wounded and bleeding. What if he should die? Was it possible he could die? She couldn't bear that. What would her life be without him?

A sudden image rose up in her mind of Stephen—*her* Stephen, the very meaning of her existence—lying unconscious and bleeding on the floor of that bank, shot through the chest, the leg. Would he be crippled for life? Would he even have a life?

Wave after wave of stark fear rolled through her, leaving her limp. She buried her face in her hands and groaned aloud. It can't be, she agonised. I won't let him die.

But he wasn't *her* Stephen any more, and she sobered instantly at the thought. Then why had he asked for her? *Had* he asked for her? Why else would Laura Blake have called her?

There was no time for speculation. All she knew was that she had to go to him, whether he wanted her or not, to see for herself how badly he was hurt. Bracing herself on the arms of the chair, she jumped to her feet. She had already wasted precious moments.

Moving swiftly now, she grabbed her handbag and ran outside to her car.

She drove through pouring rain the ten miles to Pensacola, but by the time she arrived at the hospital the sun had broken through the clouds at last, and the pavement ahead steamed from the warmth of its rays beating down.

At the reception desk on the main floor of the hospital Joanna was given the number of Stephen's room, and that was about all. In the way of tight-lipped hospital personnel the world over, the receptionist had politely refused to give her any details whatsoever about his condition.

As she stepped out of the lift on the fifth floor, she saw Laura Blake, in uniform, waiting in the small foyer, and she hurried over to her.

'How is he?' Joanna asked.

'They're operating right now,' Laura said tersely. She was obviously very upset herself, her jaw set and grim, her body held tensely erect, but was doing her best to cover it up. 'I have to leave now to go and file my report.'

Panic began to rise up in Joanna again. 'But how is he?' she insisted. 'Surely you have some idea.'

'It doesn't look good,' she said. 'You'd better talk to his doctor.' She punched the lift button viciously and turned her head away, but not before Joanna saw the tears glistening on her cheeks and the stricken look on her face.

When she was gone, Joanna ran down the wide corridor towards the nurses' station at the far end. A white-capped nurse was sitting behind the glassed-in partition. She glanced up as Joanna approached.

'Yes,' she said. 'May I help you?'

'My name is Joanna Barnes. I've come to see Stephen Ryan, the policeman who was shot.'

The nurse gave her a stern look. 'Are you a relative?'

Joanna's mind raced. She'd never get anything out of her if she told the truth, that she was really nothing to him. 'I'm his fiancée,' she said at last.

The nurse consulted her chart. 'He's still in surgery,' she said. 'After that, he'll be in intensive care for several hours. It will be some time before you'll be able to see him.'

'But how is he?'

The nurse looked past her. 'Here comes his doctor now. You can ask him yourself.'

Joanna whirled around to see a white-coated young doctor just emerging from the lift and walking slowly towards the nurses' station. She ran to him.

'I'm Stephen Ryan's fiancée,' she explained again. 'Can you tell me...?'

It was then that she saw the two orderlies behind the doctor. They were wheeling a hospital trolley out of the lift, and on it lay a long, still form that seemed to be entirely covered with white sheets. Joanna raised a hand to her mouth to stifle the cry that rose to her lips at the sight. Then she turned to the doctor again.

'Is he...?' She couldn't go on.

'No,' the doctor said wearily. 'He's still alive. We're taking him to intensive care now, where he'll be very closely monitored for the next few hours.'

He motioned to the two orderlies, who began to push the trolley out of the lift, and she had one awful glimpse of the man lying beneath the white sheet. His face was ashen, a terrible pale grey, drained of any trace of colour. The features looked drawn and haggard, and there was no sign of life or breath in the still form.

As she gazed down at him, a terrible blackness closed down on her. An unpleasant tingling sensation crept along the surface of her skin, and the next thing she knew, her knees buckled under her and she was falling—falling—falling.

'Miss Barnes. Joanna. Are you all right?'

Joanna opened her eyes and blinked at the face leaning over her. It was the young doctor. The nurse she had spoken to earlier was hovering behind him, a long needle in her hand.

'Where am I?' she murmured. 'What happened?'

Then she remembered. Stephen's lifeless form, the shock of seeing that pale, ashen face, then— blankness. She must have fainted, passed out cold right in the corridor.

'Oh,' she said. 'I'm so sorry.' She struggled up on the couch and gave the doctor an apologetic look. 'I'm sorry to be so much trouble,' she said again. 'I've never fainted before in my life.'

The doctor smiled. 'It happens often in hospitals. We get used to it.'

'Stephen,' she said. 'Lieutenant Ryan. Is he dead?'

'No, of course not,' he said with another smile. 'Believe me, we wouldn't have brought him up here if he were.' Then the smile faded, and he frowned at her. 'But he's very weak.'

'Will he be all right?'

'It's too soon to tell. The bullet in his chest punctured a lung, and the one in his thigh grazed a large bone. We had to go into both his chest and his leg to remove the bullets and repair cartilage and blood vessels, and that's an extremely traumatic insult to the human body. He also lost quite a lot of blood. We had to give him six pints on the operating-table.'

'When will you know?'

'He'll be in intensive care until——' he glanced at his watch '—late this evening at the earliest. His vital signs—heart, blood-pressure, brain activity—are being closely monitored. He'll have constant care by our best nurses. If all goes well, he'll be out of danger tonight.'

'*If* all goes well?' she asked in a quavering voice.

The doctor rose to his feet and looked down at her sternly. 'We've done all we can for him. We're *doing* all we can for him. There are limits to what medical science can accomplish, however. You must try to understand and be patient.'

'Can I see him?'

'I wouldn't advise it now. You saw what he looked like out in the corridor. It won't improve until he can move around, get some nourishment. My advice to you is to go home, try to get some rest, then give us a call later tonight. We'll know more by then.'

Joanna stood up and faced the doctor. Their heights were just about even, and she gazed straight into his eyes. 'I'd like to see him now,' she said firmly. 'I promise I won't faint again. But I must see him. Just for a minute. Please.'

Somehow she felt compelled to do this, to prove to herself that she could face it, as though to make up for her previous weakness. She was filled with shame at what she had done, passing out like that at the first sight of him.

The doctor shrugged. 'All right,' he said. 'But just for a few minutes.'

She picked up her handbag and followed him out of the room. As they walked down the wide, highly waxed, spotless corridor, he spoke to her in a low voice. 'You'll have to wear a mask. There's a terrible danger of infection after serious surgery like that. It's another reason why we need to keep him isolated for several hours. Give the body a chance to recuperate from the trauma.'

They had come to a door at the far end of the corridor on which the words 'Intensive Care' were printed in bold black letters. The doctor opened the door, then stood aside to let Joanna enter.

'I'll leave you now,' he said, handing her a mask that he had picked up from a table near the door.

'Mrs Parker will answer any questions for you. But be brief. Just a few minutes.'

He left her then. Joanna tied the mask over her face, stepped inside the room and shut the door behind her.

An efficient-looking nurse with a starched uniform and greying hair sat beside the bed, her eyes firmly fixed on a row of complex machines that beeped at regular intervals. As Joanna watched, the nurse took Stephen's wrist in hers and glanced at the watch on her arm, obviously taking his pulse.

When she was through, she glanced up at Joanna, who was still standing transfixed just inside the door staring down at the narrow bed. All she could think of was that this motionless form was Stephen. Yet it couldn't be. Stephen was so real, so full of life, so strong. It was as though she had been given a complex equation to solve and wasn't even able to grasp the bare essentials of it.

Once again, blackness threatened. She couldn't stay in that awful room another moment. She was just about to whirl around and run for the door when she heard a low moan coming from the still form lying on the bed. She turned to look at him, and her own fears were forgotten at the sight of him lying there so helpless.

If there was a chance in the world that he had called for her, wanted her to come to him, she couldn't let him down now. She'd stick it out, for his sake, for the sake of the love she still bore for him. But most of all, she grasped dimly, for her own self-respect.

She gave the nurse a brief nod and a smile, whispered that she'd be back later, and left the room. Outside in the corridor, she tore off the mask and took several deep, gasping breaths. Then she walked slowly down the hall to the lifts.

When she got there, Laura Blake was just getting out. The two women were alone in the wide corridor, silent and hushed except for the occasional chime and sepulchral voice calling for a doctor. The two women stared at each other, motionless, for several moments.

Then Joanna said, 'Do you have time for a cup of coffee? I'd like to hear more details about what happened.'

Laura lifted an eyebrow and gave her a long, appraising look. Once again Joanna felt the hostility emanating from her and immediately regretted her friendly impulse.

'All right,' Laura said at last. 'Shall we brave the cafeteria?'

They rode down on the lift to the basement cafeteria, which was virtually deserted now at this time of evening. The only coffee available was out of a machine, and they carried it in the flimsy paper cups to a small round table by a window.

Joanna looked down at the muddy brew with distaste, took a tentative sip, and made a face. It was barely lukewarm and hardly recognisable as coffee.

Laura laughed shortly. 'I can see you're not used to institution food,' she said, pouring cream into her own cup. 'It definitely needs doctoring. You should taste the swill we're given down at the station.' She pushed the cream pitcher across the table. 'Try this. It helps.'

Joanna poured in just enough cream to take the edge off the bitterness and took another sip. 'It's a little better,' she said with a smile.

Laura lit a cigarette, and the two women sat in an awkward strained silence for some time. Across the room a tall, stringy black man was lazily pushing a mop back and forth over the tiled floor, the soft swishing sound the only noise to be heard.

Joanna was torn between wanting to be friendly with this woman, a co-worker of Stephen's, and a deep mistrust because of the hostility she sensed in her. But most of all she was dying to ask the burning question that had etched itself in her mind.

Finally, Laura drained her coffee, dropped her cigarette in its dregs and started fiddling with the plastic spoon in her hand, drumming it on the table-top. She looked at Joanna.

'I suppose you're wondering why I called you to-night,' she said bluntly.

Joanna was taken aback by the flat statement. 'Well,' she stammered, 'I guess I thought—I mean—didn't Stephen ask for me?' she blurted out at last.

Laura laughed shortly. 'Hardly. He was uncon-scious from the moment he was hit.' She leaned forward across the table and fixed Joanna with narrowed eyes. 'Call it an act of charity,' she said coldly. 'I was almost certain he'd had it—the blood he lost, the extent of his injuries—and in a moment of weakness I decided he might want to say goodbye to you, in spite of the way you'd hurt him.'

Joanna widened her eyes in disbelief. 'The way *I* hurt *him*!' she exclaimed. 'You've got your facts twisted. It was Stephen who put an end to our re-lationship, not me.'

Laura's face twisted in a sneer. 'Oh, come, now. Are you trying to tell me that you were supportive of his job? From what I gathered, you could barely tol-erate going with him to visit his partner's widow when her husband was killed.'

Indignation rose in Joanna like a hot flame. She leaned back in her chair and eyed the other woman angrily. 'And just how do you know that?' she asked. 'Have you and Stephen been discussing me?'

To her amazement, Laura's face went up in flame, and she dropped her eyes. 'No. Stephen wouldn't do that. I just gathered as much when I asked him about it.' She looked up at Joanna again, her face miserable. 'I don't suppose it comes as any great surprise to you to hear that I was interested in Stephen myself.'

'No,' Joanna replied softly, the anger draining out of her. 'I gathered as much the first time I saw you together.'

Laura shrugged. 'There was never anything between us. I tried, believe me, but Stephen has pretty firm ideas about mixing business and pleasure. You must know how dedicated he is to his profession. And a dedicated policeman needs a personal life totally removed from his work. I think he was hoping to get that from you.'

'It wasn't the way you think,' Joanna said. 'Did you know I was married to a policeman who was killed?' Laura nodded. 'I'm not asking for sympathy,' Joanna rushed on. 'I was young and foolish then, and when Ross died I vowed I'd never get involved with a policeman again.' She shrugged. 'Then Stephen came along, and I forgot that vow. But there was still a lingering fear, and Stephen sensed that. He couldn't tolerate it. And I can't say I blame him. But I'm over that now.'

'And what makes you think that?' Laura asked brutally. 'I don't think you're cut out to be a policeman's wife. Besides, Stephen always said he'd never marry, that he'd never put that burden on any woman he cared about.'

Joanna had had enough. She picked up her empty coffee-cup, rose to her feet, and looked down at Laura. 'Thank you for calling me tonight,' she said evenly. 'I'm very grateful. But I think this is something Stephen and I will have to work out ourselves.'

Laura stared up at her. 'That's fair enough. But Stephen is my only concern. I just don't want to see him hurt.' She got up then and walked over to a nearby bin, where she tossed in her own empty cup. Then she turned and walked away, her high heels tapping on the tiled floor.

Joanna stared after her until she was out of sight, then slumped back down limply in her chair. All her bones seemed turned to jelly. As she sat there alone, for a long time, thinking over what Laura had said, wondering if she was right, the cardboard coffee-cup crumpled in her hand, and she tore napkin after napkin into shreds.

Stephen hadn't asked for her. Laura had taken it upon herself to call her. She didn't know what to do, whether to stay or go. More to the point, if she did stay, would Stephen even want to see her?

Before she could decide what to do, she'd have to find out if there was any change in his condition. She left the cafeteria and took the lift back up to the intensive care unit. There was no sign of Laura Blake. At the nurses' station she was told that Stephen was still unconscious and would probably remain so for the rest of the night.

After extracting a promise from the nurse on duty to call her if there was any change, Joanna made her way back outside to her car and drove home.

*     *     *

First thing the next morning, Joanna jumped out of bed, ran down the hall to the telephone in the living-room and called the hospital.

'Fifth floor nurses' station,' came a cheerful voice.

'This is Joanna Barnes. I'm Stephen Ryan's fiancée. How is he this morning?'

'One moment, please.' There was a short delay while the nurse consulted her chart. 'Oh, he's much better this morning, Miss Barnes. Of course he's still in a lot of pain and heavily sedated, but he did regain con-sciousness, and that's the important thing.'

'Is he still in intensive care?'

'No. Now that he's out of danger he's been moved to a private room on the sixth floor.' She gave Joanna the number of the room.

After she'd hung up, Joanna went into the kitchen to make herself a cup of coffee. While it perked, she drank a glass of juice and dialled Edward Morgan's office number. As she hoped, Betty answered.

'Betty,' she said hurriedly, 'I called to tell you that I'm going to have to take some time off. I don't know how long. A couple of days, anyway.' She took a deep breath. 'Stephen's been hurt. He was shot. He's in the hospital at Pensacola, and——' Her voice broke.

'Hey, hold on, honey,' Betty said. 'Let me get this straight. I thought you and he—I mean, I'm sorry he was hurt, but does this mean you two have patched things up?'

'Oh, Betty, I don't know,' Joanna wailed, still fighting back tears. 'I hope so. I have to run now. Will you see if Edward or Andy can cover for me for a few days?'

'Sure, honey. And give Stephen our best.'

Back in the kitchen, Joanna poured herself a cup of coffee and gulped it down at the counter. When she was through she rinsed out her cup, then ran down the hall to her bedroom to get dressed.

Inside the hospital she was greeted by that familiar sickening smell, and she hurried towards the lifts. On the sixth floor, she stood for a moment outside Stephen's room to compose herself, then pushed open the door and stepped inside.

The blinds at the window were pulled shut, and the room was dim and cool. Stephen was lying on a narrow bed, his long, motionless form outlined under the white covers, his dark head turned to one side. He was wearing a hospital gown, and his bare arms lay beside him outside the blanket.

'Stephen,' she called softly as she approached the bed.

He turned his head and looked up at her groggily. The blue eyes were dull and glazed over, but as they focused on her he smiled weakly and moved a hand towards her. She sat down on the chair beside the bed and reached for his hand.

'Sorry about this,' he mumbled thickly. 'Stupid of me to get shot.'

She leaned over him to kiss his forehead. It felt feverish, hot and damp. She smoothed back the dark hair. 'How do you feel?' she asked in a low voice.

'A little out of it at the moment.' His fingers curled around her hand, and he smiled again. 'I understand my fiancée was here last night. Do you know her?'

Joanna flushed crimson. 'Stephen, about that...'

The fingers tightened. 'I like that,' he said sleepily. 'It has a nice ring to it.'

He closed his eyes then as a spasm of pain crossed his face. Joanna's heart went out to him, not only for the physical pain he had to endure, but for his helpless condition. She knew how he would hate that. If only there was something she could do for him. Should she call the nurse? She couldn't bear to see him suffer.

Gazing down at him now, at the broad shoulders barely covered by the scanty gown, the long column of his neck, the hollow at the base of his throat where a little pulse throbbed, the finely drawn features, the shadowy black stubble on his firm jaw and strong chin, she felt that she had never loved him so much as she did at that moment.

She sat that way for some time, holding his hand, stroking his face. Once or twice his eyes opened, and he would look up at her, as though to reassure himself she was still there, then they closed again as he drifted back into a drugged half-sleep.

The nurse she had spoken to last night came inside just then, another long needle in her hand. She smiled at Joanna and went to Stephen's side.

'It's time for his shot,' she explained. 'He'll be unconscious for several hours. He needs sleep more than anything else right now, and we'll keep him sedated until tomorrow morning. There's really no point in your coming back until then.'

Joanna got up and thanked the nurse, then, with one last look at the man in the bed, left the room and went back out into the hall. She felt profoundly relieved at his improved condition. It could have been so much worse, she thought as she walked slowly to the bank of lifts. He could have been killed.

For the next few days, Joanna spent as much time at the hospital with Stephen as she was allowed. Each day he grew stronger, and each day he became more impatient and irritable at the confinement.

'I simply don't see the point,' he grumbled on the third day. 'I'd be just as well off at home. I'm perfectly capable of looking after myself now.'

'They want to make sure you're healing properly and there's no infection, Stephen,' Joanna explained patiently for the twentieth time. 'You don't want to have to go through all this again, do you?'

He was sitting up in bed dressed in a new pair of pyjamas Joanna had bought for him, and a robe she had picked up at his house. He looked like a small boy to her, and oddly vulnerable with the tousled dark hair falling over his forehead and the dark scowl of annoyance darkening his fine features.

He glared at her. 'I know that. I just hate this damned inactivity.'

Although from the beginning he had seemed to accept her presence there without question, as time went on he also seemed to withdraw more from her. After that first morning, in fact, when he had just regained consciousness, he seemed almost to resent her presence. He certainly hadn't shown her any affection since then, or even any interest in whether she showed up or not.

She knew he was anxious to get back on the job. On several of her visits to him there had been various members of the police force there, both in uniform and out, and the talk was always of current cases and how badly they needed Stephen back on regular duty.

'Well,' she said, 'when your stitches come out tomorrow, that'll all be over and you'll at least be able to move around a bit.'

He didn't even bother to reply. He just lit a cigarette and gave her another disgusted look.

Just then there was a commotion at the door and Karen Morgan burst in. She ran to Stephen's side, threw herself on the bed and started sobbing hysterically.

'Oh, Stephen, darling,' she cried. 'I just found out what happened. Why didn't you call me? I've been out of my mind with worry and came the minute I heard about it. Are you all right? Is there anything I can do for you?'

Embarrassed by the ridiculous display, Joanna turned her head away. She felt like a spare part. At least he hadn't called Karen and asked her to come rushing to his side, any more than he had Joanna herself.

She glanced over at the bed. Karen was sitting on it now, still crying quietly, but apparently a little calmer now. Joanna watched as the girl smoothed back Stephen's dark hair and leaned down to kiss him on the cheek. Although she couldn't see Stephen's face, he didn't seem to be making any strenuous effort to stop her or resist her gushing ministrations.

Joanna rose to her feet and cleared her throat noisily. 'I guess I'll go down to the cafeteria to get some breakfast,' she said.

When neither of them looked around, she turned and started to walk out of the room. Before she reached the door, however, she heard Stephen's voice, loud and clear.

'For Pete's sake, Karen,' he bellowed. 'Will you please stop that blubbering and get off me? You're leaning on my bad shoulder.'

Startled by the angry tone, Joanna turned around. Karen had drawn back from him and was looking down at him with a hurt expression on her face.

'I'm sorry, darling,' she said, pouting prettily. 'I didn't mean to hurt you. I thought you'd be glad to see me. I want to take care of you.'

'I don't need you to take care of me,' he roared.
'Now get off the bed, please, and leave me alone.'

Slowly, the girl stood up. With a toss of her long
bright mane, she put her hands on her hips and looked
down at Stephen, who was still glowering darkly up
at her and rearranging the bandage she had disturbed.

'Stephen,' Karen said with a feeble attempt at
dignity, 'I don't understand why you're behaving this
way. I came rushing over here, all prepared to——'

'Just get out of here, will you, Karen?' he ground
out. 'I already told you. I don't want you here. I don't
need you. Now, please leave.'

Karen turned then and started towards the door,
darting Joanna a dirty look as she went. When she
was gone, the door closed behind her, Joanna started
to walk towards the bed. Although she couldn't help
feeling a little sorry for Karen at the brutal way
Stephen had rejected her, she was also secretly pleased
that he didn't want her.

As she approached, he looked up from the dressing,
which was now back in place, and the smile died on
her lips when she saw that his face was still dark with
anger.

'That goes for you, too, Joanna,' he said coldly. 'I
don't need you and your hysterics, either. Just leave
me alone.'

She gazed down at him, stunned at the harsh words.
She reached out a hand to touch him, but he brushed
it away. The cold, remote look on his face sent chills
down her spine. His distance, his detachment from
her, made her feel as though he was disappearing
before her very eyes.

'Stephen, I don't understand,' she faltered. 'I
thought you were glad to have me here.'

'I never asked you to come, did I?'

'Well, no, but I thought when Laura Blake called me...'

'Laura had no business doing that,' he said flatly. 'I've already had that out with her.'

Her heart was thudding painfully against her ribs. Somehow she had to make him understand that she'd changed, that she could face up to the dangers of his job with courage from now on. She willed herself to stay calm.

'Have I had hysterics, Stephen?'

'I understand you fainted the first night you came,' he stated flatly. 'I don't know what you call that, but it sounds very much like hysterics to me.'

'But that was only because I was so worried about you!' she cried. 'I've been fine since then.'

For a moment the cold gaze faltered, and she thought she could detect a tiny spark of warmth in the brilliant blue eyes. But then the dark look was back.

'It's no use, Joanna,' he said in a dull tone. 'I want you to go. And I don't want you to come back. I simply can't take it.'

He turned his head away from her and gazed stonily out the window.

He meant it. There wasn't a shadow of a doubt in her mind about that. She could stay and plead with him forever, beg, make a scene, but in the end she knew she couldn't win out over that iron determination. The powerful will she had so admired in him was now her enemy, and she had no defence, no weapon against it.

She picked up her handbag from the floor and walked slowly towards the door. It seemed like a million miles, and at each one she hesitated, hoping he would change his mind, call to her, tell her it was a mistake.

But the summons never came. Eventually, after what seemed like hours, she reached the door, opened it and went outside into the corridor.

# CHAPTER TEN

'HE DOESN'T want me,' Joanna said. 'He made that perfectly clear last week.'

Betty put her hands on her plump, corseted hips and glared at her. 'And you believe him?'

The argument had been raging for half an hour. Joanna had called the hospital that morning, just as she had every single day during the past week since Stephen had sent her away, and had been told he was being released that afternoon.

'Betty, what am I supposed to do? Walk into his room and calmly announce I'm going to take him home?'

'Why not?'

'Because he doesn't *want* me, that's why! How many times do I have to tell you that?'

Betty gave her a pitying look. 'If you believe that, you'll believe anything. You'd be out of your mind not to give it another shot. He was hardly out of the anaesthetic when he said that. Even though he'd never admit it, having such a close call must have shaken him badly. He just took it out on you. And,' she added with a grin, 'poor Karen. Although I'm not sorry to see her get her come-uppance at last. She's been sulking ever since he ordered her out of his room, and the last I heard is making noises about going back to Miami. Which for my money can't be too soon.'

Joanna had to smile at that.

'Besides,' Betty went on, 'what have you got to lose? A little pride, that's all. But if you don't give it one

173

more try you'll lose far more than that. You'll be giving up your last chance at the man you love, the man who really loves you but who is too pig-headed to admit it.'

'He *was* wrong about me,' Joanna said slowly, feeling herself weakening. 'I didn't go to pieces when he was hurt. At least I proved it to myself that I could face up to it.'

'Right. Now, go and prove it to him.'

In the end, of course, Joanna had to admit Betty had a point. The worst he could do was tell her to leave. Still, that afternoon when she stepped off the hospital lift at the sixth floor and started walking down the corridor towards his room she was trembling with nervous anticipation, her knees constantly threatening to buckle under her.

What was worse, when she reached his door, she saw Laura Blake standing there talking to Stephen's nurse. The tall blonde was out of uniform today, and wearing a good-looking pink linen dress that hugged her slim figure in all the right places and made her look like a million dollars.

Joanna's heart sank when she saw her, and she hesitated for a moment. But then she kept on, her head held high, ready to do battle. As she approached, Laura looked up and their eyes met.

'I've come to take Stephen home,' Joanna announced firmly. She turned to the nurse. 'Is he ready?'

The nurse looked from one woman to the other, clearly bewildered. Then, apparently deciding to let them fight it out for themselves, she shrugged and said, 'Yes. I'm just going now to get a wheelchair for him. Hospital policy, you know,' she added cheerfully, 'in spite of the fuss he's making about it.'

When she was gone, Laura and Joanna continued to stand and stare at each other for several moments. Joanna was determined not to back down now that she'd come this far, and her gaze never wavered.

It was Laura who finally looked away. She gazed off into the distance for a moment, as though thinking it over, then turned back to give Joanna a crooked smile.

'You know,' she said softly, 'if I thought there was one chance in hell he'd turn to me with you out of the picture, I'd fight you to the death. But I know that's not in the cards. I'll give you your innings, mainly because I'm so certain you'll fail him. And when you do,' she added fiercely, 'I'll be there to pick up the pieces. By then he might be glad to have me.'

She turned and strode away down the hall. Joanna stood there looking after her, shaken by the encounter, but still determined to go through with what she had come here to do. She opened the door and walked into Stephen's room.

He was standing in the middle of the room in his pyjamas and dressing-gown, leaning on a pair of crutches and stuffing his belongings into the flight bag sitting on the bed. When he looked up to see her standing in the doorway, his face clouded over, and as she walked towards him the frown deepened.

'What are you doing here?' he said at last.

'I came to take you home.'

'What happened to Laura?'

'She—er—she decided to leave.'

One corner of his mouth quirked up briefly, and for a moment she was certain he was going to smile, but in the next instant it was gone, and he only nodded. Well, she thought, at least he hasn't kicked me out—yet.

'How are you?' she said briskly. 'You're looking well.'

He was, too. The grey look was gone, and he had all his old colour back. He was freshly shaved, his hair combed neatly, and she longed to reach out to him, to take him in her arms. But she restrained herself and instead walked purposefully over to the bed and picked up his bag.

'I'm fine,' he said, 'except for wanting to get out of this damned place.'

'Are you sure you feel up to it?'

The nurse came in just then, pushing a wheelchair before her. 'I felt up to it days ago,' he said irritably. 'They tell me I have to leave in this thing,' he grumbled, pointing at the offending wheelchair. 'I'm perfectly capable of managing by myself on the crutches.'

'Hospital regulations, Lieutenant Ryan,' the nurse said in her most officious manner.

They finally got him wheeled outside and into Joanna's car, and once they were on their way Stephen leaned back and expelled a long sigh. 'Am I glad to get out of that place.'

They drove the rest of the way without speaking. Stephen seemed content just to gaze out the window at the passing scenery, and Joanna concentrated on her driving. The silence between them was awkward, even unnerving. The gulf that had widened between them seemed impassable, all the lovely closeness gone, and Joanna felt a dead weight of hopelessness settle over her.

At his house, he did manage to negotiate quite well on his crutches while Joanna carried in his flight bag. Once inside, he sank down on the couch in the living-room with a sigh of relief.

'It must seem good to be home again,' she said with a shaky smile. 'Are you hungry? Can I get you something to eat? Perhaps you're tired. That was quite a heroic effort getting into the house on those crutches. Would you like to lie down for a while? I haven't had time to do any shopping, but——'

'Joanna!' His harsh voice broke in.

She had been standing by the fireplace as she spoke, twisting a handkerchief in her hands, her eyes darting around the room, anywhere but into his eyes. Now, at his curt tone, her hands stilled and she had to look at him.

'I don't need a nursemaid,' he said. 'I can manage quite well on my own from now on.'

'I see,' she said. 'What about food?'

'Laura saw to that yesterday.'

'Oh.' She glanced down at her feet, uncertain what to do. Then, when he remained stonily silent, she looked up and said, 'Well, I guess I'll be on my way, then.' She started to walk slowly over to the door.

'Joanna,' he called to her when she reached it. She turned around to face him. 'Thanks for the ride home.'

Well, that was something, wasn't it? Just a slight wedge, but infinitely better than cold silence. He probably just wanted to be alone in his own home for a while.

'That's all right,' she said. 'I was happy to do it.' Once again she hesitated, then gritted her teeth and forged ahead. 'I'll come back later to fix you some supper and see how you're making out.'

Before he could object, she hurried out the door.

For the next week Joanna came faithfully every day to Stephen's house to take care of him. She had vacation time coming to her from her job, and now that

Edward Morgan was entirely recovered he was able to manage the hotel on his own anyway.

After the first awkward day, a pattern became established. She would drive over first thing in the morning to fix his breakfast, and while he ate she would make his bed and straighten up the place. His cleaning woman still came on schedule that week to do the heavy cleaning and take care of his laundry. He was basically a neat man in any case, and all Joanna really had to do was to prepare his meals and go the grocery shopping.

At first, she was happy to do these things for him, delighted that he even allowed it, but after five days of it she began to give up hope that her care of him would make any difference to their relationship. His manner towards her remained frosty, as though he was merely tolerating her presence.

In the beginning, she had attributed his silent withdrawal to the fact that he'd been badly hurt and was still recuperating. Although he managed quite well now on his crutches, he was a very bad patient, sullen and moody. But gradually, as the days passed, it became clearer to her that she was only there on sufferance, that he neither enjoyed nor appreciated her company, and by the end of the week she was ready to throw in the towel and give it up as a bad job.

That day he had been particularly obnoxious. She'd made his breakfast and he'd hobbled in from the bedroom in his old dressing-gown, unshaven and morose, his black hair tangled. He sat down silently before the bacon and eggs she had prepared for him, and irritably snapped open the morning paper with a loud crackle.

Joanna was standing at the kitchen counter, her back to him, pouring out his coffee, and at the sound the muscles along her back, her arms, her shoulders clenched into knots. Tears stung her eyes, tears of self-pity and her growing sense of hopelessness, but most of all now of sheer resentment and frustration.

She banged the mug down on the counter so hard that a good portion of hot coffee splashed over the rim on to her arm, scalding it painfully. With a sharp cry, she turned on the cold water tap, let the cool water run over the burned arm for a few seconds, then wrapped a towel around it.

It was the last straw. Tears streaming openly and unchecked down her face, she whirled around to face him. The sight of him sitting there calmly eating the meal *she* had cooked for him, his eyes firmly fixed on the newspaper by the side of his plate, his slovenly appearance, were all suddenly too much for her.

She unwrapped the towel from around her arm, threw it on the floor and stamped her foot. 'Look at you!' she cried, making a sweeping gesture to encompass the whole distasteful scene.

His head came up slowly and he stared blankly at her, a piece of toast still in his hand. 'I beg your pardon,' he said calmly.

This only escalated her fury. 'You ought to take a good look at yourself,' she went on with rising passion. 'You've been slopping around here for a week in that filthy old bathrobe, and I'm sick of it. You can't even get dressed, you don't shave, I wonder if you even bathe or brush your teeth!'

The blue gaze narrowed and a thunderous look crossed his face. 'In case you hadn't realised it,' he said in a tone of hurt dignity, 'I'm only a week out of hospital.'

'Oh, I realised all right. Why else do you think I'm here?'

He laid his fork down carefully on his plate. 'I don't know, Joanna. Why are you here?'

'I honestly couldn't tell you that any more, Stephen. I thought I was here to help you, because you needed me, but it's become quite obvious now even to thick-headed me that you don't want me here. You've treated me like a servant ever since I brought you home. No, worse than a servant. Worse than a *dog*, even.' Her voice rose hysterically with each word she uttered.

He had risen slowly to his feet during her impassioned recitation of grievances, and stood there now, leaning on his crutch, his face black with barely suppressed rage.

'If you'll recall,' he snapped, 'I didn't ask you to come. You hatched that little scheme all by yourself. I didn't want you here in the first place. I thought I'd made that clear.'

He was right. Suddenly all the anger left her. She felt unutterably weary. It was hopeless. It had been from the beginning. She should never have listened to Betty.

'Yes,' she said dully. 'I do recall.'

She stooped down and picked up the towel, mopped up the spilled coffee with it, then got up and rinsed it out at the sink. All her muscles seemed to be made of lead. It was as though she was trying to swim through mud, and the simple chore seemed to take forever. When she finally hung the wet towel neatly over the draining-board, she turned back to him. He hadn't moved, and his face was totally devoid of expression, flat and unyielding.

'The real reason I came, Stephen,' she said in a low voice, 'was to try to prove to you that you were wrong about me, that I had grown out of my childish fears, that I could be a good policeman's wife now. And that I'd rather suffer ten times that old anxiety than lose the man I loved.' She shrugged hopelessly. 'I was wrong. I think now that there was another, deeper reason for your rejection of me, perhaps a hidden fear of your own, a fear of commitment maybe, and that can be just as crippling as my old fear of danger.'

During her speech his expression hadn't altered by a hair, and, when she was through, she crossed over to the sideboard near the door where she had set down her handbag. She picked it up, then continued towards the doorway.

Without looking at him, she said, 'I'm going now. I won't bother you again. I'm sure Karen Morgan or Laura Blake will be happy to come and look after you. You don't need me, and it's clear to me at last that you certainly don't want me.'

She went out through the doorway then, still hoping in her heart of hearts he might stop her even now, but he made no sign and spoke no word.

That evening, Joanna took a long walk on the beach. It was during the dinner hour, and most of the guests were up in the hotel dining-room, so that she had the sands virtually to herself.

She'd leave Miramar, she decided as she trudged along through the squeaky white sand. She couldn't stay here now. Perhaps Edward could convince Karen not to leave after all, and she could stay and take over. If not, Andy Thompson was coming along nicely, and with a little guidance could probably do the job himself.

She'd miss it, the clear, sparkling water, the mild, balmy climate, the job she'd worked so hard at, the people she'd come to care for. Perhaps she'd try

Miami, or California. She didn't think she could go back to Boston, with its cold, snowy winters, its crowds and congested traffic.

She stayed out until the tourists began straggling down to the beach for one last evening swim. It had begun to grow dark by now, and as she approached her cottage she noticed that she had left a light burning in the living-room. That was careless, and not like her, she thought, as she walked slowly up the steps.

She opened the door and went inside, then stopped dead in her tracks. There, sitting on the couch in the living-room, was Stephen. He was dressed in a pair of dark trousers and a clean white shirt, open at the collar. He was freshly shaven, his black hair a little too long, but combed neatly, and the only reminder of his recent illness was the pair of crutches leaning against the arm of the couch. At the sight of him, her heart began to pound painfully.

'How did you get here?' she asked when she could speak.

'I called Betty,' he said quietly. 'She came to get me.'

Clasping her hands before her, she walked over to the window and stood staring out into the gathering dusk. There were still faint streaks of red over the far horizon. From the beach below came the sound of children's voices raised in shouts and laughter.

Finally she turned around to face him. 'Why did you come?'

He scowled and looked down at his feet. 'I came to apologise to you, for one thing,' he muttered. 'I've behaved like a pig this past week, and I'm sorry.'

'All right,' she said. 'Fair enough. Apology accepted. Is Betty going to drive you home?'

He raised his head and gave her a long bleak look. 'I'm not finished,' he said at last. He took a deep breath. 'The main reason I came was to admit to you that I was wrong about you. I think that deep down I knew it all along. And you were right, there *was* a deeper reason why I put up those barriers between us.' He ran his fingers through his dark hair. 'I don't know if I can explain.'

As she gazed at his transformed appearance and listened to the tone of genuine humility in his voice, a ray of hope began to flicker in Joanna's heart. But, fearful that she might only be kidding herself, she tried hard to fight it down.

She crossed the room to the couch and stood before him, looking down at him, aching with all her heart to reach down and take him in her arms, but she was still too uncertain of his intent. Perhaps he'd only come to make his apologies as the prelude to a final farewell, and when he was sure he was forgiven he'd get up and leave, walk out of her life forever.

'Please,' he said, gazing up at her, 'will you sit down beside me?'

She hesitated for a moment. 'All right,' she said, and lowered herself slowly on to the couch next to him, close, but not touching.

He began speaking in a low voice. 'At first, when you raised the subject of my going back to the law, it troubled me, but I didn't really blame you after your bad experience in the past. But then, when you reacted so violently on that visit to my dead partner's widow, I became convinced it would never work between us.'

'I couldn't help that, Stephen,' she said quietly. 'And I'm sorry for my weakness. I just wasn't ready.'

He nodded. 'I see that now, but that day I didn't have the sense to realise that and to be patient. At the time, I honestly felt it was best to call off our relationship before it was too late. Best for you and for me. Your reaction only confirmed my conviction that most women can't tolerate being tied to a policeman, that eventually they panic and run. I couldn't face the thought of a future worrying about you sitting at home having nightmares every time I was out on a job.'

'But I didn't panic and run when you were hurt, did I, Stephen?' she asked.

He turned to face her. 'No, Joanna,' he said. 'You didn't. But by then I'd actually been shot myself. I didn't know whether I'd live or die, and I admit I was frightened. Stubborn, too,' he added with a sigh. 'I'd made my stand, and I wasn't going to back down.' He put his hands on her face and tilted her head up so he could gaze into her eyes. 'It hurt like hell to give you up,' he said softly. 'I was crazily in love with you, and still am. But once I'd made the decision, I felt I had to stick to it.' He smiled bleakly. 'Sheer male pride, I guess.'

She wanted to tell him it didn't matter, that it was all in the past, that now they could make a fresh start, but something held her back. He wasn't through. She folded her hands in her lap and waited, holding her breath for what was coming.

'It's not important now, anyway,' he said at last. He took in a deep lungful of air. 'I've decided to leave my job.'

She stared at him, dumbfounded. It was the last thing in the world she had expected. 'Stephen, you can't do that!' she cried without thinking. 'You love your work. You've always been so positive, so certain you would never give it up. What made you change your mind?'

He shrugged. 'It's quite simple. I finally came to the conclusion that no job is worth losing you. If I have to make a choice, it's got to be you. I love you, Joanna. I want to marry you, if you'll still have me.'

'You'd do that for me?'

'Yes, but it's more than that.'

'What else, then?'

He rubbed a hand over the back of his neck and shook his head slowly. 'I'm not sure. Several things, I guess. Getting hurt forced me to examine my life more deeply, to decide what it was I really wanted. I had a lot of time to think, lying in the damned hospital bed.' His hand moved to her hair. 'But most of all it was you. Quite simply, I didn't want to lose you. You brought a warmth into my life that I never knew existed.'

'Then why did you send me away today?' she asked.

'Because I didn't really grasp that fact until after you'd gone, and there I was alone in a house with all the light and joy taken out of it, left with nothing by my stupid pride. Then I knew that a life without you was a life without meaning, no life at all, and no job is that important.'

'Oh, Stephen,' she said, 'I do love you. I always have. And I want to marry you. But I can't ask you to do that. You'd be miserable without the work you love.'

He shook his head. 'No,' he said. 'I'd be miserable without you. It'll work itself out, you'll see.'

'Look,' she said, 'I can't promise I won't always worry about you, but you've got to give me a chance. The important thing is that we try, that we trust each other. And so long as we're together, anything is possible.'

As his brilliant blue eyes bored into hers, she prayed silently. Oh, please, he's got to agree to try. She knew with absolute conviction that, if he gave up his work for her sake, eventually he would come to resent her for it.

Finally he put out a hand to touch her on the cheek. 'All right, darling,' he said with a smile. 'If you're game, I guess I am, too.'

She leaned towards him then and his strong arms came around her, sheltering, protective. Pressing herself up against him, she raised her face to his. As his mouth came down on hers in a long, probing kiss, she slid her hands up over his chest, the taut, firm muscles rippling under her eager fingers, and then around his neck.

His hand came down to rest on her breast, slipping inside the opening of her dress to caress her bare skin. He tore his mouth from hers and looked down at her, the blue, blue eyes glazed over with desire.

'I love you, Joanna,' he muttered hoarsely.

Joanna felt as though her heart would burst with joy. She rose slowly from the couch and held out a hand to him.

'Come,' she said, and they walked slowly together down the hall to her bedroom.

Later, after he had made slow, passionate love to her and they lay side by side in her bed, Joanna turned to him.

'Stephen,' she murmured lazily, 'you said earlier that your fear I wouldn't be able to handle your job wasn't the only reason you became convinced it wouldn't work between us. You never did really explain that.'

He thought a moment. 'At the time I thought so,' he said at last. He propped himself up on one elbow and gazed down at her. 'All right. It was probably partly just an excuse. I see that now. I think I half realised it at the time, but didn't want to admit it. I saw a quality in you—a strength of character—that told me you would never try to stop me from doing what I wanted to do, no matter how much you disliked it. It's one of the things that attracted me to you in the first place.' He eyed her wickedly. 'That, and your beautiful body,' he added, moving his hands over her in one long, sweeping stroke.

She caught at his searching fingers. 'Be serious,' she said. 'Then why did you send me away?'

He eyed her steadily. 'I hate to admit it, but I think I was afraid of you. Terrified would be a better word.'

'Afraid?' she asked incredulously. This brave man, who faced bullets without a qualm, afraid of her?

He sighed deeply and pulled her up against him, tucking her head under his chin and stroking her smooth hair. He was silent for a long time, and she could feel the steady beat of his heart next to hers.

'You have to understand,' he said at last. 'Warmth, love, family life—those things were totally foreign to me. We're all afraid of the unknown. I'm no exception.'

'But you're not afraid any more?'

His hold on her tightened. 'Not if you're there to love me, to teach me,' he murmured against her hair. After a short silence, he cleared his throat and said, 'Er—, Joanna, I know I have no right to ask, but was there anything between you and Martin during our separation?'

'Of course not,' she assured him heatedly. 'Martin Kingsley is a silly playboy.' She thought a minute. 'And what about you and Karen Morgan? I saw the way she hung all over you at Betty's and Edward's wedding reception.'

Stephen's lips twitched. 'Ah, Karen,' he said, leaning his head back against the pillow, a faraway look in his eyes.

Joanna sat bolt upright in bed, pulled the sheet up to her chin and glared at him. 'Yes, Karen! Just how close were you?'

'You're jealous,' he teased.

'Darned right I'm jealous!'

He reached for her again and pulled her down beside him. 'Well, you can forget that silly little twit. She just decided to follow me around, that's all, but I never laid a hand on her or gave her a passing thought.'

Joanna smiled secretly to herself. Safe in Stephen's arms, she knew now that even if her old fears returned she would work it through. Her mind turned briefly to thoughts of her dead husband. Even though she'd lost him, she wouldn't give up one moment of the short time they had spent together.

She sighed contentedly. She seemed to be destined to fall in love with men involved in danger, and you couldn't fight your own destiny. Stephen is my destiny now, she thought, with deep contentment, and turned over to nestle against the long, hard body of the man she loved.

From *New York Times* Bestselling author
Penny Jordan, a compelling novel of ruthless passion
that will mesmerize readers everywhere!

# Penny Jordan

# Silver

Real power, true power came from
Rothwell. And Charles vowed to have it,
the earldom and all that went with it.

Silver vowed to destroy Charles, just as surely and
uncaringly as he had destroyed her father; just as he had
intended to destroy her. She needed him to want her . . .
to desire her . . . until he'd do anything to have her.

But first she needed a tutor: a man who wanted no one.
*He* would help her bait the trap.

Played out on a glittering international stage,
Silver's story leads her from the luxurious comfort of
British aristocracy into the depths of adventure,
passion and danger.

**AVAILABLE IN OCTOBER!**

 **HARLEQUIN**

# Take 4 bestselling love stories FREE

## Plus get a FREE surprise gift!

# PASSPORT TO ROMANCE
# SWEEPSTAKES RULES

1. **HOW TO ENTER:** To enter, you must be the age of majority and complete the official entry form, or print your name, address, telephone number and age on a plain piece of paper and mail to: Passport to Romance, P.O. Box 9056, Buffalo, NY 14269-9056. No mechanically reproduced entries accepted.

2. All entries must be received by the CONTEST CLOSING DATE, DECEMBER 31, 1990 TO BE ELIGIBLE.

3. **THE PRIZES:** There will be ten (10) Grand Prizes awarded, each consisting of a choice of a trip for two people from the following list:
   i) London, England (approximate retail value $5,050 U.S.)
   ii) England, Wales and Scotland (approximate retail value $6,400 U.S.)
   iii) Carribean Cruise (approximate retail value $7,300 U.S.)
   iv) Hawaii (approximate retail value $9,550 U.S.)
   v) Greek Island Cruise in the Mediterranean (approximate retail value $12,250 U.S.)
   vi) France (approximate retail value $7,300 U.S.)

4. Any winner may choose to receive any trip or a cash alternative prize of $5,000.00 U.S. in lieu of the trip.

5. **GENERAL RULES:** Odds of winning depend on number of entries received.

6. A random draw will be made by Nielsen Promotion Services, an independent judging organization, on January 29, 1991, in Buffalo, NY, at 11:30 a.m. from all eligible entries received on or before the Contest Closing Date.

7. Any Canadian entrants who are selected must correctly answer a time-limited, mathematical skill-testing question in order to win.

8. Full contest rules may be obtained by sending a stamped, self-addressed envelope to: "Passport to Romance Rules Request", P.O. Box 9998, Saint John, New Brunswick, Canada E2L 4N4.

9. Quebec residents may submit any litigation respecting the conduct and awarding of a prize in this contest to the Régie des loteries et courses du Québec.

10. Payment of taxes other than air and hotel taxes is the sole responsibility of the winner.

11. Void where prohibited by law.

## COUPON BOOKLET OFFER TERMS

To receive your Free travel-savings coupon booklets, complete the mail-in Offer Certificate on the preceeding page, including the necessary number of proofs-of-purchase, and mail to: Passport to Romance, P.O. Box 9057, Buffalo, NY 14269-9057. The coupon booklets include savings on travel-related products such as car rentals, hotels, cruises, flowers and restaurants. Some restrictions apply. The offer is available in the United States and Canada. Requests must be postmarked by January 25, 1991. Only proofs-of-purchase from specially marked "Passport to Romance" Harlequin® or Silhouette® books will be accepted. The offer certificate must accompany your request and may not be reproduced in any manner. Offer void where prohibited or restricted by law. LIMIT FOUR COUPON BOOKLETS PER NAME, FAMILY, GROUP, ORGANIZATION OR ADDRESS. Please allow up to 8 weeks after receipt of order for shipment. Enter quickly as quantities are limited. Unfulfilled mail-in offer requests will receive free Harlequin® or Silhouette® books (not previously available in retail stores), in quantities equal to the number of proofs-of-purchase required for Levels One to Four, as applicable.

## OFFICIAL SWEEPSTAKES
## ENTRY FORM

Complete and return this Entry Form immediately—the more Entry Forms you submit, the better your chances of winning!
- Entry Forms must be received by **December 31, 1990**
- A random draw will take place on **January 29, 1991**                    3-HP-1-SW
- Trip must be taken by **December 31, 1991**

YES, I want to win a PASSPORT TO ROMANCE vacation for two! I understand the prize includes round-trip air fare, accommodation and a daily spending allowance.

Name_____

Address_____

City_____ State_____ Zip_____

Telephone Number_____ Age_____

Return entries to: **PASSPORT TO ROMANCE**, P.O. Box 9056, Buffalo, NY 14269-9056

© 1990 Harlequin Enterprises Limited

## COUPON BOOKLET/OFFER CERTIFICATE

| Item | LEVEL ONE Booklet 1 | LEVEL TWO Booklet 1 & 2 | LEVEL THREE Booklet 1, 2 & 3 | LEVEL FOUR Booklet 1, 2, 3 & 4 |
|---|---|---|---|---|
| Booklet 1 = $100+ | $100+ | $100+ | $100+ | $100+ |
| Booklet 2 = $200+ | | $200+ | $200+ | $200+ |
| Booklet 3 = $300+ | | | $300+ | $300+ |
| Booklet 4 = $400+ | | | | $400+ |
| Approximate Total Value of Savings | $100+ | $300+ | $600+ | $1,000+ |
| # of Proofs of Purchase Required | 4 | 6 | 12 | 18 |
| Check One | | | | |

Name_____

Address_____

City_____ State_____ Zip_____

Return Offer Certificates to: **PASSPORT TO ROMANCE**, P.O. Box 9057, Buffalo, NY 14269-9057

Requests must be postmarked by **January 25, 1991**

✂

## ONE PROOF OF PURCHASE                    3-HP-1

To collect your free coupon booklet you must include the necessary number of proofs-of-purchase with a properly completed Offer Certificate

© 1990 Harlequin Enterprises Limited

See previous page for details